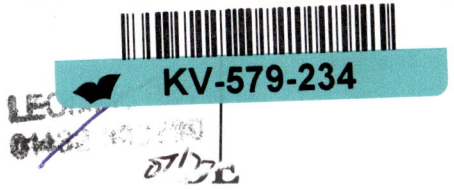

Perry Hamil, a fugitive from Texas, is headed for the Canadian border. Riding through Montana, he witnesses the massacre of a stagecoach and all its passengers by the Sioux — and when he investigates what's left, he's inspired with an idea. What if one of the five mutilated bodies were . . . him? No more wanted posters or crazy gunfights. No more threat of the gallows. So Perry becomes Barry Rodman, a young Virginian who'd been bound for Bozeman to inherit a fortune — more money than he's ever dreamed of. All he has to do is wait around for six months. But Barry's fiancée is keen to come stake her claim on her man. And Harry De Shon, a trigger-happy sheriff, knows Perry from the old days. Both are headed for Bozeman — and it won't take them six months to get there!

SPECIAL MESSAGE TO READERS

THE ULVERSCROFT FOUNDATION
(registered UK charity number 264873)
was established in 1972 to provide funds for
research, diagnosis and treatment of eye diseases.
Examples of major projects funded by
the Ulverscroft Foundation are:-

- The Children's Eye Unit at Moorfields Eye Hospital, London
- The Ulverscroft Children's Eye Unit at Great Ormond Street Hospital for Sick Children
- Funding research into eye diseases and treatment at the Department of Ophthalmology, University of Leicester
- The Ulverscroft Vision Research Group, Institute of Child Health
- Twin operating theatres at the Western Ophthalmic Hospital, London
- The Chair of Ophthalmology at the Royal Australian College of Ophthalmologists

You can help further the work of the Foundation
by making a donation or leaving a legacy.
Every contribution is gratefully received. If you
would like to help support the Foundation or
require further information, please contact:

**THE ULVERSCROFT FOUNDATION
The Green, Bradgate Road, Anstey
Leicester LE7 7FU, England
Tel: (0116) 236 4325**

website: www.ulverscroft-foundation.org.uk

MONTANA MASQUERADE

ALLAN VAUGHAN ELSTON

SAGEBRUSH
Large Print Westerns

First published in Great Britain by Ward Lock
First published in the United States by Lippincott

First Isis Edition
published 2021
by arrangement with
Golden West Literary Agency

A catalogue record for this book is available
from the British Library.

ISBN 978–1–78541–866–2

Published by
Ulverscroft Limited
Anstey, Leicestershire

Set by Words & Graphics Ltd.
Anstey, Leicestershire
Printed and bound in Great Britain by
TJ Books Ltd., Padstow, Cornwall

This book is printed on acid-free paper

Remembering two bold pathfinders, Jim Bridger and John Bozeman, who nearly a hundred years ago blazed rival trails to the Gallatin Valley of Montana, scene of this book

CHAPTER
ONE

From long habit Perry Hamil stopped on the bluff's rim to look cautiously ahead. It was the same, always when he rode into a new town or entered a strange room. Right now, Canada-bound and a fugitive from Texas, there was really no need for it. This was Montana where he was unknown, and where there was hardly a chance of running into an old enemy on either side of the law.

Riding north across New Mexico from El Paso, he'd seen more than a few "man wanted" posters each offering a reward for Perry Hamil, gambler, road agent, killer — "white, male, twenty-six, hair and eyes brown, usually well dressed, smooth-shaven, handsome, dangerous." Such notices had petered out in southern Colorado. In upper Colorado and in Wyoming he'd put up at hotels without serious risk. And now, a thousand miles north of El Paso, Perry Hamil reined up on the rim of a bluff purely because reconnaissance of every new scene had become second nature.

What he saw was the broad, grassy valley of the lower Yellowstone River in eastern Montana. Along it he could see no settlement or ranch. Nor any railroad, for

1

this was June, 1880, with the end of Northern Pacific rails still somewhere in Dakota.

The only life in sight was a small herd of buffalo grazing a mile or so beyond the river. A stage road followed the river whose water was at June tide, high enough for navigation of the small steamers and flat-bottomed mackinaws which sometimes plied along it as far as Benson's Landing, more than two hundred miles to the west. Just now no river craft was in sight.

Nothing was in sight except those buffalo — and all at once the animals began moving. Fast! Up went their heads and they made off at a thundering run toward the north. Hamil wondered what had frightened them. He'd stopped just short of the bluffs rim and nothing more than his head could be seen from the river valley; not enough to stampede buffalo nearly three miles away.

Then, east up the stage road, a four-horse coach came in sight. Its wheels made dust on the riverbank. Yet Perry Hamil was still mildly puzzled. The buffalo had begun running a full minute before the stage hove in sight.

As he watched the stage rumble westward, a mood of discontent came to Hamil. Canada would be a cold, lonely place. He'd a hundred times rather be riding that stage west to Bozeman, or to the gold fields of Virginia City and Bannack. Yet he couldn't risk it. As a hunted man with his neck at stake, he must push on north across the border.

The stage bore nearer and Hamil, waiting for it to pass, wondered who was on it. Homeseeking immigrants, probably. Hamil had studied maps and knew the routes they'd have to travel. A train to the end of rails, then a boat up the Missouri to the mouth of the Yellowstone, then a smaller boat up the Yellowstone to Miles City, only a few miles east of here. Then by stage up the Yellowstone and on over Bozeman Pass to Bozeman, in the Gallatin Valley.

Bozeman, end of the West's longest and most famous cattle trail! Always Perry Hamil had wanted to go there. As a boy he'd seen many great herds leave Texas, heading for Montana via the trail blazed by John Bozeman; later he'd seen those trailsmen return home, telling tales about Bozeman in a valley of green grass and rushing rivers, circled by walls of snowy mountains.

As he watched the stagecoach a rebellious envy teased Hamil. Sixty hours from now, after changing teams perhaps twenty times, that stage would be in Bozeman . . .

Whoops and rifle fire broke abruptly on Hamil's thought. He saw a band of thirty-odd Sioux Indians jump its ponies from a coulee on open prairie beyond the river. With savage yells the band bore down on the stage.

The driver lashed his horses to a gallop. But Hamil, watching from the bluff, knew it was no use. That west-bound stage, and everyone on it, was doomed. Four harnessed horses could never outrun those ponies, or the bullets which blazed from their ruthless riders. The Indians were gaining, closing in fast. The

3

driver was already hit. Hamil saw him collapse on the forward boot.

It was all over but the looting and the scalping. And Hamil himself would share the same fate if they spotted him here on the bluff. He drew back out of sight, dismounted, tied his horse to a sage bush. No use running for it till he picked the right direction. It must be opposite to whatever direction the Indians took, after the raid.

Presently Hamil crawled belly-down back to the bluff's rim and peered over it. The river was a mile away with the stage road on its farther bank. The stage, driverless, had come to a halt. A circle of mounted savages nearly hid it from Hamil's sight. The shooting and yelling had stopped; and the clear reason for it brought a creeping of flesh to Hamil's spine. It meant that the butchery had already taken place.

They were slashing harness from the stage horses. They'd be sure to make off with the horses; and perhaps with money from the wallets of passengers, because money could be traded for firearms and whisky.

Prone on the bluff, Hamil waited only to see the direction of retreat. If it was east he'd go west; if west he'd go east. If it was south toward him, they'd first have to swim their mounts across the river.

The raid itself didn't much surprise him. For this was between the mouth of the Tongue and the mouth of the Rosebud. Less than fifty miles from this spot, four years ago this June, General George Custer and his entire command had been massacred by Sioux and

4

Cheyenne. All the world knew that. This very neck of the range had been the hot spot of that bloody Sioux war.

The Sioux war was over now — but an occasional spark still flew upward from its ashes. Sitting Bull and his head chiefs had been rounded up, their teeth drawn, but a few small renegade bands, fiercely spiteful, still roamed Montana. They'd sniped off many a lone hunter, burned many an isolated ranch, looted many a stage coach on the Miles City-to-Bozeman line. Some of those deadly bands had been run to earth by cavalry; but a few others, after a quick strike, had always managed to disappear into some trackless crack in the mountains.

This was such a band and presently Perry Hamil saw it ride away from its crime. The Indians rode west up river leading the four stage horses.

No life stirred about the stage which, oddly, hadn't been set afire. Perhaps because the raiders hadn't wanted a column of smoke to advertise the raid. A wagon train might be coming along any minute; or even a detachment of cavalry on routine patrol from Fort Keogh.

Hamil made no move till the raiders had faded from sight. Then, mounting his horse, he spurred it down the bluff's slope to the valley level. From there, partly because it was his original direction, and partly to count casualties, he rode straight toward the looted coach.

Arriving at the river, he swam his horse across it. The north bank was like the south, treeless, prairie sod reaching to the brim. In this sod the wheels of traffic had cut deep ruts. Many a covered wagon had passed here. In the deepest of the ruts stood the teamless stage, its driver sprawled across the seat.

Perry Hamil had seen death many times before, had dealt it himself, and was hardened to it. But here was a picture to freeze the blood. There'd been four passengers, all male; three had been dragged outside and one still remained in his seat. Like the driver, all four were riddled with bullets, scalped and hideously mutilated.

Hamil averted his eyes. "Let's get outa here!" He kneed his mount and headed on north toward Canada. As for reporting the raid, let the first passing wagoner do that. No use getting embroiled himself . . .

Yet a sudden bold idea made Perry Hamil wheel his horse and again face the ravaged coach. Five men lay dead there, each mutilated beyond recognition. What if one of those five were himself, Perry Hamil?

The same shadowy thought had come to him a year ago, down on the Pecos in Texas. He'd shrugged it away then. Now it returned, with an insidious challenge, to tempt him again.

Down on the Pecos, while hiding, out from the rangers, he'd come upon the partially decomposed body of a man. Identity and cause of death unknown. Hamil's thought had been to plant upon it his own watch, luck ring, spurs and wallet. Then let it be found and identified as the hunted outlaw, Perry Hamil.

It would hush a hue and cry, and halt the hunt for Hamil. He could ride on to some faraway range and begin a new life, unhunted. And a hundred "man wanted" posters, describing him, would be removed from post office walls.

He'd dismissed the idea mainly because the casualty had been too long dead, and Hamil himself had been seen alive only a month earlier. Yet during this past year the possibilities had returned to tease and haunt him. Some day he might again chance upon a dead man. If so, what positive and convincing identifications could be planted?

What more than his watch, luck ring, spurs and wallet? What about a batch of IOU's accumulated from various gaming tables in Texas, all payable to Perry Hamil? They'd be no good to a fugitive in Canada. But a vague idea of using them as proof of his own death had kept Hamil from destroying them. They were in his wallet right now. What if they were found on one of these five massacred men?

Hamil dismounted, moved nearer to look them over. The driver couldn't be considered. He'd be well known at both ends of his run. So Hamil gave attention only to the four passengers.

The first was clearly too old, more than twice the age of Perry Hamil. The second was too fat, the third much too short.

The fourth body was inside the coach. Its scalped head was bloody and its face hacked to ribbons; but this didn't hide the brownness of the eyes nor the six-foot length of body. Unwrinkled skin made the man look fairly young. His boots had no spurs and his clothes didn't look Western. A portmanteau on the rack over his head suggested that he was a stranger to this range and had traveled a long way.

A wallet lay at his feet where the raiders had dropped it. Only money had been taken from it. Still in it was a one-way stage ticket from Miles City to Bozeman.

Bozeman! A name to conjure with and one which had always attracted Hamil. Except that he was a hunted man, he might be going there himself. What else did this passenger have on him?

A pocket of the wallet had cards and receipts; also the stub of a ticket recently used for steamer passage up the Missouri River. A rent receipt from a boardinghouse in Roanoke, Virginia, was made out to Barry Rodman. Probably that boardinghouse had been the traveler's last address; also it suggested that he had no family, because family men rarely live in boardinghouses.

Another likelihood struck Hamil. The one-wayness of the tickets indicated that Barry Rodman had come west to stay.

How long had he lingered in Miles City between boat and stage? Had he talked about himself there? Had the stage agent, in selling him a ticket, made a record of his name?

A dozen uncertainties struck Hamil. If he went through with it he'd be taking a terrific gamble. But Hamil was a gambler by trade. If he made this throw and won, Perry Hamil the outlaw would no longer exist. Under a new name he could ride on into a new life. He could forget Canada and head west, toward Oregon or California.

It was a decision he couldn't dally over. Hamil got out of the stage and looked warily both ways along the trail. No wagon or rider was in sight. Sound came only from the sluggish current of the river.

Three times in as many minutes Perry Hamil changed his mind. He would! He wouldn't! His gambler's chin took a fatalistic set as he got back into the stage. He'd do it! He looked at a portmanteau on a rack over the seat. He must heave it into the river and leave his own saddle roll in its place.

First he traded watches with Barry Rodman and put his own garnet luck ring on a dead finger. A hundred Texas barrooms had seen that ring on a swift sure hand dealing cards. He took the jacket off Rodman and substituted his own, and buckled his heavy, Mexican spurs on the man's boots. Dropping his own high-crowned hat, with the label of an El Paso merchant on the sweatband, he picked up a flat, black hat bought in Virginia by Barry Rodman.

He put the stage ticket to Bozeman in his own wallet and dropped the wallet at the dead man's feet. In it were IOU's payable to Perry Hamil. He kept his money, since the raiders had taken Rodman's. Last he traded belts. The one he buckled on Rodman was a money belt, empty now except for a pair of trick dice.

When he got out of the stage the Texan was wearing Rodman's jacket and hat. An inner pocket of the jacket had papers but there was no time to look at them now. The important thing was that nothing was left on the body to identify it as Rodman's, and much was there to identify it as Hamil's. His own saddled horse, waiting

9

cock-kneed by the trail, brought another idea to Hamil. The horse had a Texas brand and he'd stolen it at El Paso. If he turned it loose near Miles City, they'd think the thief had abandoned it there to catch a stage for Bozeman.

Hamil picked up the portmanteau to heave it into the river. Then it occurred to him that in late fall, when the river was low, the bag might show above the riffles and be dragged ashore. So he'd better carry the thing a long way off and burn it.

Hamil balanced the bag back of his cantle and tied it there. His own saddle roll, with a forty-five gun wrapped in it, he planted in a rack of the stagecoach. The gun itself, with its notched bone butt, would make the most convincing identification of all.

Riding north across the open prairie, Hamil missed that gun. In all his adult life this was the first time he'd ever ridden a range unarmed. The bulky bag back of his cantle added to his sense of awkwardness. At the first water hole he'd build a campfire and burn it.

What else was there to get rid of? This horse, for one thing. After turning it loose, he'd walk into Miles City to buy another.

The real weakness of the deception was, he admitted, that while he'd planted himself on the stage he'd failed to account for the disappearance of Barry Rodman. Rodman would have friends in Virginia who knew he'd journeyed to Bozeman. Maybe someone was waiting to meet him at Bozeman. When he didn't show up they'd want to know why.

They'd be able to trace his travels by train and river boat as far as Miles City, Montana. Maybe a stage agent would remember selling him a ticket to Bozeman. Hamil licked a cigaret, broodingly. Ten to one his trick wouldn't pan out. The one favorable chance was that Rodman's Virginia friends wouldn't become alarmed until he failed to report his arrival at Bozeman. By the time a tracer got as far as Miles City, the five stage victims would be a month buried. A month in the fast roaring life of Miles City — already known as "the Cowboy Capital of the West" — its streets and hotels and bars milling with strangers, immigrants, gamblers, nameless adventurers. Who then would remember for certain just what stranger had boarded a certain stage on a certain day in June. As for a certain stage-raid victim, the record would say he was an outlaw named Hamil, now buried, and whose stolen horse had been picked up near town.

With a gambler's shrug Hamil rode on north. At the worst his trick would be exposed and he'd have to keep on riding, riding . . .

Presently he struck Sunday Creek and camped there. The place was about fifteen miles north of the stage road and the same distance northwest of Miles City. A cottonwood windfall offered fuel and he made a fire. His saddlebags still had a crust of bread and a ration of jerky.

He washed at the creek and then tried to scrub bloodstains from the jacket he wore. They were worse than he'd thought and he gave it up. When his fire was hot enough he'd burn it, along with the portmanteau.

It was nearly nightfall, while Hamil was smoking an after-supper cigaret, when he remembered an envelope in the jacket's inner pocket. He picked up the jacket and probed curiously.

Three papers were in the envelope. The first was an honorable discharge from the U.S. Navy. It was dated two months ago at Norfolk, Virginia, and made out to Barry Rodman of Roanoke.

The second was a formal letter of introduction signed by the president of a Roanoke bank, presenting the bearer, Barry Rodman, to Davis & Davis, a law firm of Bozeman, Montana.

At this point Hamil grimaced and wished he'd kept clear away from that raided stage. If Rodman was important to bankers and lawyers, his identity wasn't to be trifled with.

Then Hamil read the third paper. It was a letter dated six weeks ago, addressed to Barry Rodman of Roanoke, written on the engraved stationery of Davis & Davis.

Needles of excitement pricked Hamil.

. . . as attorneys for your late uncle, John Rodman of this city, we herewith notify you of his decease and the terms of his will. His estate is left to his only surviving relative, yourself. It consists mainly of a well-stocked cattle ranch in this country, a brick business block on Main Street in Bozeman and an account in the Gallatin County Bank.

We are filing the will for probate and we assume that you, in due course, will arrive to accept possession of the estate.

Before his decease your uncle informed us that you have recently served an enlistment in the Navy. When you come to Bozeman, and purely as a formality, we suggest that you bring along the following papers of identification:

(a) your discharge from the Navy

(b) this letter

(c) a letter of introduction from a Roanoke bank

(d) any letter addressed to you in the hand of John Rodman

The will names this firm as executors. Any preference you may have as to operation of the estate, pending probate, will be duly considered. In the meantime we remain

your obedient servants,

Davis & Davis, Attorneys
by *Wilbur Davis*

Hamil read it again. And again. Three of the identifications were already at hand. What about (d), a letter from uncle to nephew?

Barry Rodman's portmanteau lay by the fire. Perry Hamil opened it, sifted through it for a letter signed by the Bozeman cattleman, John Rodman.

Two were there, one dated just before Christmas of 1878, and one at Christmas of 1879. Each had enclosed a check for ten dollars. A quick reading told Hamil that the uncle had never seen the nephew since infancy. Therefore he couldn't have described Barry Rodman to the lawyers.

A well-stocked cattle ranch! A brick business block! A bank account! All for Barry Rodman!

So why not let Barry Rodman have it? And at the same time prevent a hue and cry about his disappearance?

It was still a gamble. But the stakes were really worth playing for now. For Barry Rodman could still arrive on a stage at Bozeman — in the person of Perry Hamil.

CHAPTER
TWO

Hamil kept the portmanteau, burning only the stained jacket. An hour after nightfall he saddled up and rode down Sunday Creek. By midnight he sighted the lights of Miles City. When they were less than a mile away he dismounted. It took only a minute to remove saddle, bridle and baggage from the horse. Then he turned the animal loose.

Saddle and bridle he hid in a sage bush. Then he picked up Barry Rodman's portmanteau and walked across a river bridge into town. Only the main street was noisy and lighted. Hamil kept in the dark of a back street till he found a cheap rooming house. A sleepy woman there rented him an upstairs room. The name he signed on her book was Jim Brown.

He slept twelve hours and it was past noon when excited talk from the street wakened him. He heard galloping hooves. Looking out a window he saw a troop of cavalry pound along Main Street, a block away, and march westerly out of town. Men bunched on the walks, some with rifles in hand. The air was full of questions and grim answers.

"Where did it happen, Bill?"

"About twenty-two mile up the river."

"How many were on it?"

"Five. Tom Eukes was drivin'. They just took him to the morgue."

"Him and who else?"

"The Bard brothers from Forsyth and Jess Bixby. Other guy was some stranger named Hamil."

Hamil listened in alert suspense for the name Barry Rodman. Any mention of that name would be his cue to run far and fast. His masquerade was sure to fail if there was any immediate inquiry about Rodman.

Hearing none, Perry Hamil dressed and went down to the street. At the first store he bought a corduroy jacket, much like the one he'd burned last night. Wearing it, and with Barry Rodman's flat black hat low over his eyes, he leaned against a saloon wall with an ear to the sidewalk talk. Most of it was about yesterday's raid.

"Where's the stage station?" Hamil asked a lounger.

The man thumbed to the right. "Two blocks west, mister. Right next to Wells-Fargo."

Hamil approached it from the opposite side of the street. In front of it a crowd was circled about the looted stagecoach. Relief teams had hauled it into town. "Enough slugs in it," a man muttered, "to salt a lead mine."

"Damn them varmints! Reckon the troopers'll ketch 'em, Dave?"

"If they do it'll be the first time," Dave said bitterly.

Hamil turned in at a restaurant across from them, took a front-window table and ordered. All through it he listened to comment from the street. The stage agent and two deputies were in the crowd. And still Hamil heard no mention of the name Rodman.

The only names he heard were Eukes, Bard, Bixby and Hamil.

After eating, the Texan crossed to the stage office. At the front was a newsstand and an express counter. Stage schedules and tariffs were posted on a wall. Hamil saw that the westbound stage left daily at six A.M. A one-way passage to Bozeman was priced at eight dollars.

Perry Hamil bought a paper and sat on a bench. It was last week's issue and the news was stale. Pretending to read, Hamil listened to talk from customers and clerks. This morning's stage for the west, he learned, had left on time. Troopers were patroling the road and there was no danger from Indians. "They never strike twice in the same place," a man said. "Next time you hear of 'em they'll be hackin' up a wagon train t'other side of the divide."

A customer came in, dressed for travel. He stopped at the ticket window. "One seat to Bozeman, please, on tomorrow's stage."

The agent gave him a wry smile. "Sorry. We're sold out two weeks in advance."

The fact jarred Hamil. It seemed to mean that Barry Rodman, in order to get a seat on yesterday's stage, must have waited here two weeks. In that case he'd be known at a hotel.

So the masquerade was too risky! With a shrug Hamil decided to give it up. Odds against him were too big and he'd better toss in his hand. Nothing to do now but reclaim his saddle from a sage bush, buy another horse and ride on north.

That was his plan when he left the stage station. But voices on the walk stopped him. The man who'd tried to buy a ticket to Bozeman was being offered one now. "It'll cost you double, mister. Sixteen bucks. I got to make a livin', you understand."

A ticket scalper! Hamil paused to listen. Ticket scalping was common practice in railroad stations; so why couldn't stage tickets be bought and sold the same way? Often a passenger would buy a ticket and later find he couldn't use it. Then a speculator would buy it from him at a discount and sell it for a bonus.

"Too steep," this particular prospect growled. "I'll buy me a horse and join some wagon train." He moved away.

On an impulse Perry Hamil stepped up to the scalper. "If that ticket's for tomorrow's stage, I'll take it."

A minute later he walked away with a ticket to Bozeman. Maybe Barry Rodman had picked up his own the same way. If so there'd be no record of the sale.

Not that Hamil had made up his mind to use the ticket.

He could still back away from the gamble. First he must check at the hotels and at the steamboat landing.

Main Street only had two hotels worthy of the name. Their lobbies were crowded. In each room-hunters were being turned away. "We're full up," one desk clerk said. "Come around later," the other clerk suggested, "and maybe I'll have a cot in the sample room."

Hamil looked several days back on each register and failed to see Rodman's name. Probably he'd been forced to sleep at some back-street rooming house.

At the boat landing Hamil found a small steamer loading for its downriver run. *Rosebud* was the name painted on her hull.

"When did she get in?" Hamil asked a roustabout.

"Day before yesterday," the man said.

The *Rosebud* had cabin space for ten passengers. Hamil went aboard and found the mate. "I rode in to meet a friend named Thad Walker. Did he come upriver on your boat?"

"Don't think so," the mate said. "But won't take but a minute to look it up." The passenger list he took from a file had ten names on it. "Nope. We didn't fetch along anyone by the name of Walker. Maybe he'll come upriver tonight. The *Yellowstone*'s due here about dark."

"Thanks." Hamil turned away. But his eyes had swept down that list of ten names and one of them was Barry Rodman.

So Rodman had been in town only one night. One night in a back-street rooming house which he'd left at daybreak to board a westbound stage! The odds were getting shorter all the time.

But they were still risky. So Hamil went back to Main Street and moved from bar to bar. Talk was mainly about the raid. Always those same names — Eukes, Bard, Bixby and Hamil. No whisper of a passenger named Rodman.

"Who was this guy Hamil?" a bartender asked. "Can't place him."

"Texas card shark," a customer said, "judgin' by the stuff they found on him. And a bad actor, too, judgin' by a notched gun in his slicker roll. The sheriff sent out some wires to get a line on him."

In late afternoon the local paper came out. It bristled with the raid story. The coach had been brought to town and the victims identified. Four local men and a Texan named Hamil. A troop of cavalry was now pursuing the raiders up the Rosebud toward the Wolf Mountains in Wyoming.

Hamil could find no hint of mystery as to the identity of a victim. There was no mention of Barry Rodman. Telegrams had been sent to El Paso and Pecos asking if Perry Hamil was known there. Pecos was where some of the IOU's had been dated. Plenty of people knew him at both places. But he had no relatives or close friends. No one who would claim his body or bear the expense of his burial. "Good riddance!" would be the reaction of Texas lawmen; and his name would be crossed from a list of wanted men.

The last rivet of proof would be hammered home when they picked up a horse stolen in Texas and abandoned near Miles City, Montana.

It disposed neatly of Perry Hamil and left him two choices. He could be a penniless drifter named Jim Brown; or he could arrive at Bozeman as Barry Rodman, heir to a cattleman's fortune. Hamil read again the letter from Davis & Davis. It clearly said that Barry Rodman was John Rodman's "only surviving relative." Which meant no entanglements in the East; and in the West he was entirely unknown because the lawyers asked him to bring along papers of identification.

Nor would the masquerade, Hamil reasoned, need to last forever. He could be Barry Rodman only long enough to collect the estate and cash it in; after that he could move quietly on to the Coast.

Decision came and Hamil steeled himself to see it through. He'd disposed of Perry Hamil and now he must re-create Barry Rodman. He must establish Rodman's existence alive here at this very moment.

Finding another room wasn't easy. The one he finally located, at sundown, already had an occupant. But the man was a night bartender and used the bed only by day. Hamil took it and registered as Barry Rodman of Roanoke, Virginia.

When it was dark he went over to the rooming house where he'd slept the night before. There he recovered the portmanteau and lugged it to the new room on Main. He'd burned all bridges but one and now, with his lip stiff, he burned the last one. At the telegraph office he filed a telegram addressed to Davis & Davis, at Bozeman.

AM LEAVING BY STAGE FOR BOZEMAN AT SIX A.M. TOMORROW.

Relaxing at supper, Hamil looked again at his local paper to make sure he'd missed nothing. And in the social column he learned the name of one of his fellow passengers on tomorrow's stage.

Miss Lucia Ripley of Bozeman is expected to arrive tonight on the steamer *Yellowstone*. She has been attending college in the East since last September. Passage for Bozeman has been reserved for her on tomorrow's stage.

The item mildly disturbed Hamil. He'd be cooped up with a chattering girl for three days and two nights. He'd have to eat eight or nine meals with her at various stage stations up the Yellowstone. Women were likely to be curious. This one might ask questions he couldn't answer.

Hamil shrugged the girl from his mind and walked out into the night life of Miles City. Its dozen bars all had full houses. Some were cheap sawdust dumps while some had polished brass and glittering cut glass. A few had games and entertainers — cold-eyed, sleeveless dealers and short-skirted charmers.

It was like Perry Hamil to drift into the place where play was the highest and where dollars clinked fastest on the bar. It was a place whose ceiling-high backbar mirror seemed to double the width of the room. Through it rang the chants of dicemen and dealers. Cowboys, freighters, town sports and speculators crowded the bar and the games. A singing girl could hardly be heard above the talk and the rattle of chips.

Many of the men wore guns and again Perry Hamil missed his own. Unarmed, he felt a little uneasy in a spot like this. If he came face to face with some old enemy, or with a hostile sheriff, he'd be helpless.

But he must remember he was Barry Rodman. A gun on Rodman would be out of character. As long as he was Rodman, he must face the world unarmed.

He bought a mug of beer and took it to a small wall table. With Barry Rodman's flat black hat pulled low over his eyes he looked the crowd over. A girl came up and coaxed him for a drink. He brushed her aside. Tonight he must be as inconspicuous as possible. Talk was still largely about the stage massacre. In case there were any new theories, Hamil kept his ears open and his mouth shut.

A tall, dark man came in with a gun holstered low on his right thigh. He wore burnt-leather gauntlets with belt to match; but his jacket and pants were a bit threadbare, as though the man had seen better days. For a moment something about his long, bony face startled Hamil.

He had a vague sense of having seen the man before. Not in Texas, but somewhere else and a long time ago. The man's eyes brushed over him with no sign of interest. Then he took his place at midbar and ordered whisky.

His entrance had brought a hush over the room. Hamil saw the bartender whisper covertly to a pair of customers. Yet the man didn't look dangerous. His face was relaxed as he beckoned a bar girl and asked her to drink with him.

"Not with *you*, Harry, tonight. And you'd better go home yourself." The girl scurried out of sight.

The barman spoke uneasily. "She's right, Harry. Vard Jones was in here, looking for you. Said he'd be back later."

Harry squinted through his drink. "So you think I ought to run? No thanks. Running's not my style. I'm not looking for Vard. But I'm not hiding from him either."

The man nearest Harry backed away a little. "If Vard comes in, it'll be you or him, Harry."

Harry shrugged. "I hope not."

"He's sore as a boiled owl, Harry, about those four aces you held over his kings last night. Claims it was a marked deck.

"It was a house deck." Harry drowned his drink and bought another one. Then he stood at ease with his back to the bar, elbows hooked on it, his gun butt about six inches under his dangling right hand. The door, through which Vard Jones might come, was to his left; but he didn't even look that way.

Hamil watched him covertly. Again the man's eyes met his own without hint of interest or recognition. But this time Perry Hamil placed him. De Shon! Harry De Shon of Dodge City, Kansas!

But he doesn't remember me! How could he, after five years?

What was Harry De Shon, who back in 1875 had been a notorious town marshal in Kansas, doing here in Montana? Hamil could hardly forget his one brief brush with the man. He'd come up with a trail herd from Texas. After loading the cattle on cars at Dodge, then the end of Santa Fe rails, the boys had put on a spree at a bar. Warned that the town marshal was coming to break it up, all but three of the Texas crew had climbed saddles and hit for camp. But Perry Hamil and two others were too drunk to run. So Marshal De Shon had picked them up and kept them in his tank overnight. Next day he'd escorted them to the edge of town, handed them back their guns and told them to keep going.

Naturally Perry Hamil, barely of age at the time, would remember that contact with a celebrity like Harry De Shon. As a trail-town marshal, De Shon had ranked with Hickok and Bat Masterson. Later, a few news items about him had seeped down to Texas. Marshal De Shon had become a little too quick with his trigger; after killing a half-dozen men he'd been fired from his job.

And judging by his threadbare jacket, it hadn't been too easy to get another.

A man entered at the front; a man with trouble in his eyes. His shirt was open at his hairy throat and his hand lay on the grip of a gun.

"Your number's up, De Shon!" His threat and his draw were fast. De Shon, making no threat, matched his speed. Hamil saw a holster tip as the Kansan shot from the thigh. The two shots blotted each other and glass crashed from the backbar mirror.

De Shon had stooped slightly to make the thigh shot but now he was erect again. The whisky glass was still in his left hand. An awed whisper buzzed down the bar. "Didja see that? He didn't spill a drop!"

Vard Jones lay face down on the floor. When he didn't move, Hamil sensed he was dead.

Almost at once the county sheriff came in with two deputies. They'd been patroling the Main Street walks. "Here you are, Sheriff," De Shon said amiably, and handed over his gun, butt first.

The officer glared at it a moment, then his gaze swept over a roomful of witnesses. "Who started it?" he demanded.

"Vard did. Vard came in agunnin'. He said Your number's up, and pulled his gun."

A dozen eyewitnesses made the same statement. The sheriff gave a helpless shrug. "Means we can't convict you, De Shon. Be a waste of taxpayer money if we brought you to trial. All I can do is run you out of town."

"What for?"

"For the general peace of the county," the sheriff said. "Trouble follows you like a shadow, De Shon. You've been a peace officer yourself, so you ought to know what I mean."

To Hamil's surprise the Kansan gave in promptly. "I reckon you're right, Sheriff. I usta do the same thing myself, down at Dodge. Run trouble out of town. Which direction you want me to go?"

"Take your pick, De Shon." The sheriff took the ex-marshal's arm and marched him out, followed by one of the deputies. The other was kneeling by the dead man. Final words from the sheriff drifted back. "You can have your gun, De Shon, at the town limits. All you've got to do is keep going." Boot thumps faded down the walk.

Perry Hamil remembered something and it brought a wryness to his lips. That bone-handled gun he'd planted on a dead man, in the stagecoach yesterday! It was exactly the same gun which Town Marshal De Shon had held overnight in a jail, five years ago in Kansas. Only there'd been no notches on it then.

Hamil was up and out on the street at daybreak. He carried the portmanteau to the eating place across from the stage station. During breakfast he watched them load mail and express on the Bozeman stage. Its four-horse team stood in the traces, ready for its run to the first change station.

As the hands of a clock drew near to six, Hamil saw four passengers arrive to embark. The first was a soldier returning to one of the upriver army posts after a furlough. He climbed to a seat beside the driver. The second was middle-aged and looked like a well-to-do merchant.

The third passenger, arriving in a hack, was a red-haired girl whose ruffled skirt seemed as wide as the stage itself. Her bonnet and traveling cape looked expensive, and her leather trunk had to be roped to the roof of the coach.

Hamil picked up his portmanteau and walked over there. "Might as well hoist this up too." He handed the portmanteau to the driver, at the same time flashing a ticket in the palm of his hand. "Bozeman," he murmured, and squeezed into the coach with the three who'd preceded him. The last of these three was a young, suntanned cowboy whose baggage, consisting mainly of a stock saddle, was now strapped on a rack at the coach's rear.

It was another ten minutes before the roof baggage was secure. The stage driver looked in with a reassuring grin. "Don't worry about Injuns, miss. We got cavalry ridin' the road all the way to Billings." He climbed to his seat and slapped the reins. "Giddap!"

As the coach began moving, Hamil gave a sigh of relief. He was off without a challenge.

Then a voice hailed them from behind. Hamil heard a running pursuit. "Hold on a minute, driver!"

The driver pulled to a stop to let the runner catch up. An out-of-breath man appeared at a coach window. "Does anyone of you gents," he asked, "call himself Barry Rodman?"

For six heartbeats Perry Hamil was on the point of jumping out to make a run for it. What else could this be but a challenge? Something or someone had turned up. Some acquaintance Barry Rodman had made during his overnight stop here; perhaps someone who'd actually seen Rodman off on the stage.

"Not me," the middle-aged man said.

"Not me," the young cowboy echoed.

The girl, saying nothing, fixed curious eyes on Perry Hamil. It put Hamil in a corner and gave him no choice. "I'm Rodman," he said hollowly.

"Telegram for you." The man outside handed in a yellow envelope.

"Giddap!" Again the driver slapped his reins and again the stage moved out. Hamil opened the telegram and saw that it had arrived during the night from Bozeman. It was an answer to his own message.

BARRY RODMAN
MILES CITY
   WELCOME TO BOZEMAN. HAVE RESERVED ROOM FOR YOU AT THE LACLEDE HOTEL HERE AND WILL MEET YOUR STAGE ON ARRIVAL.
                                DAVIS & DAVIS

CHAPTER
THREE

Rolfe Kendall sat cater-cornered from the girl as the big Concord coach rattled across the bridge and turned west up the Yellowstone. His guess was that she was an army girl on the way home to husband or father. Her hatpin was a design of crossed sabres and he knew that the 2nd Cavalry was stationed at Fort Ellis, near Bozeman.

The tall, brown-haired man facing Rolfe was rereading his telegram. The fourth inside passenger, chubby and double-chinned, spoke in a friendly voice. "No bad news, I hope."

The man facing Rolfe hardly heard him. An intense absorption on his face puzzled Kendall. The wheels bumped over a rock and the jolt bounced the girl against the man's elbow. She righted herself with a smile. "Sorry." This time the man made a response. "It's a rough trail." His eyes were still on the telegram.

"And a long one," the chubby man added, "if you're going as far as I am. Won't always be this way, thank God. Three years from now we'll be riding rails up this river." He turned to Rolfe Kendall. "How far are you going, young man?"

Actually Rolfe had no definite destination. Tending cattle was his trade and his last employer, over in Dakota, had shifted from cattle to sheep. Whereupon Rolfe Kendall had picked up his saddle and boarded an upriver steamer. "Wherever the grass grows green," he answered lightly.

The girl with the cavalry hatpin gave him a quick look, half curious, faintly envious. "A man can do that," she said. "But a woman can't. Her course is plotted in advance. Home; school; work; home again. She can't drift at will, like a ship or a man."

"She's better off that way, Lucia," the chubby man suggested.

"Perhaps, Mr. Cram. But she has a lot less fun."

"Lucia and I are neighbors," Mr. Cram explained. "She lives at Fort Ellis and I'm in the feed business at Bozeman."

His inquiring look compelled self-introductions from the others. "My name's Rolfe Kendall."

The man sitting beside Lucia Ripley was less prompt to answer. "I'm Barry Rodman," he murmured finally, and again. Rolfe sensed a note of restraint. But the name brought quick reactions from Cram and the girl.

"From Virginia?" the girl asked.

"Don't tell me you're John Rodman's nephew!" Cram exclaimed. "Well, well, One of my best customers, John was. Sold him ten wagonloads of oats, winter before last, to see him through that freeze. And last fall I bought half his hay crop. You aiming to take over his ranch?"

"Whatever seems best, Mr. Cram."

"If you want my advice," the merchant went on shrewdly, "you'll hang on to that property. Both the Rodman Block and the JR ranch. Why? Because Bozeman's on the edge of a rip-snorting boom. If you don't believe me, ask Wilbur and Ridley Davis. You know them, I suppose?"

"You mean Davis and Davis, the lawyers? I've been in touch with them, naturally. They sent me this telegram."

"Anything I can do for you," Cram offered, "just speak up."

"You'll keep Walter Mason on, I hope?" This from the army girl.

"Walt Mason," Cram explained, "is the JR foreman. He's off on spring roundup right now, so he won't be meeting your stage."

The man in the flat black hat gave a self-deprecating smile. "Being a tenderfoot from Virginia," he murmured, "I'm not very well posted on roundups." He turned to the girl. "Maybe you can educate me a little, so I won't seem quite so dumb when I get to Bozeman."

Rolfe fixed shrewd eyes on the man. *If that guy's a tender-foot, then I'm a Chinaman. Just playing modest, likely, to make time with the girl.* She had a nice mouth and soft, trusting eyes, he noticed, and was well worth making time with.

"Your uncle," she explained to the man beside her, "belonged to the Gallatin Valley Stockgrowers' Association. They meet in May each year to fix a date

32

for the roundup, to elect a roundup captain, and to decide how many riders each brand must furnish."

"This year," Cram put in, "they ordered the drive to begin at the mouth of Sixteen Mile Creek on June first. They elected Peter Le Beau captain."

"But Walt Mason," Lucy said, "got almost as many votes."

Cram dropped a broad wink toward Rolfe. "She's a mite partial to Walt. If I remember right, he beaued her around all last summer."

Lucia ignored him and went on. "The five biggest outfits have to send two men each; smaller brands only send one man. Walt wrote me about it; he said he and Mack Boyd are repping for the JR this year. That's your ranch, Mr. Rodman."

"I'm learning fast. Thanks."

"The four other big cattlemen," the girl said, "are Anceney, Dilworth, Lockhart and Story. Mr. Anceney has the Flying D, west of the West Gallatin. They say he controls four hundred thousand acres."

Again the broad wink from Cram. "She seems pretty well posted, for a girl who's been East all winter."

Two hours out of Miles City they changed horses and behind fresh teams rolled on toward Rosebud. Rolfe Kendall felt excluded from the talk. Knowing nothing about Bozeman, he couldn't join in coaching Barry Rodman about the life there.

From the stage window he looked out at the broad brown current of the Yellowstone. They were never far from its bank. Beyond it, to the south, grasslands stretched on to a blue horizon. Occasionally he saw cattle; once he saw buffalo and many times he glimpsed antelope. But hardly any ranches. Settlers were keeping away from this tragic neck of the range. Memory of what had happened on the Little Big Horn, only four years back, was still too fresh.

The stage jerked to a stop. Rolfe saw a trooper and a deputy standing by the trail, each with a handful of brass rifle shells. "Hi, Dave," the driver called down. "What kind of guns did they have?"

"Repeaters," he was told grimly. "The latest army models. It happened right here, Charlie."

The driver spat into the dust. "If you ketch whoever sold 'em them guns, I hope you hang him a mile high. Giddap!"

As the stage moved on, Cram explained. "Right after they wiped out Custer, four years ago, we passed a law making it a crime for any trader to sell or trade firearms to Indians. But it looks like somebody kept right on doing it."

It was noon when they reached the mouth of the Rosebud River. After a stop for lunch at the Rosebud station, four fresh horses were hooked up. "We change teams eighteen times," Cram remarked, "between Miles City and Bozeman. It's two hundred and ninety miles."

— A third change was at Forsyth and the fourth was at the supper stop, Sanders. A new driver came on there.

Beyond Sanders, darkness fell and Rolfe Kendall napped a few hours. He was asleep at the next station and didn't waken till the one after that, which was the big army post at Fort Pease. They were now at the

34

mouth of the Big Horn and a hundred miles from Miles City.

The soldier who'd been on furlough got off and a new passenger took his place beside the driver. Lucia Ripley and Adam Cram were asleep. But Barry Rodman, Rolfe sensed, was wide awake. Camp lights winked from the dark and Rolfe heard a tramp of feet as the guard changed.

The breakfast stop was fifteen miles farther on, at Pompey's Pillar. Day had dawned. Some time during the night they'd crossed to the south bank of the Yellowstone.

The station man's wife took Lucia to her room and the girl reappeared looking fresh and beautiful. The man she knew as Barry Rodman seemed clearly aware of it. "How do you stand it," he asked, "riding day and night on a stage?"

She laughed. "In summertime it's not so bad. You should try it in winter, with sleet driving in on you and the ruts full of slushy snow."

Soon they were rolling, with still another driver on the box now. The sheepman sharing it with him had an uneasy question. "How's the ford at Huntley?"

"A bit better than hub deep," the driver said. "Reckon I can make it all right. I've done it before in June water."

Those in the coach heard and Cram offered a reassuring comment. "After we cross at Huntley we stay on the north bank all the way."

"My father had to cross seven times," Lucia remembered, "on the rescue expedition four years ago."

"He sure did," Adam Cram said grimly. "Don't reckon anyone in Bozeman'll ever forget that two-hundred-mile march across ice and snow."

"What happened?" Rolfe asked curiously.

"It was February of '76 and seven men came limping into Bozeman. They'd come two hundred miles from Fort Pease and were half frozen. They said the Fort Pease stockade was surrounded by Sioux and only forty-nine of the garrison were still alive. And they wouldn't last long unless rescued. So General Brisbin took the force at Fort Ellis, crossed Bozeman Pass and marched down the Yellowstone, fording it seven times in blizzard weather. When they got to Fort Pease only nineteen of the garrison were still breathing. They were taken back to Bozeman. Lucia's dad was a troop commander on that march."

"They abandoned Fort Pease," Lucia said, "leaving nothing there but the flag and one gun. That was in March. The Custer battle was three months later."

"It was a ticklish season," Cram remembered, "for us at Bozeman. With nearly all the Fort Ellis troops gone, we'd've been easy prey for the Indians. But I guess they were too busy butcherin' folks on the Big Horn."

In a little while the driver shouted back to them. "This is it! Hold on tight, everybody."

Rolfe looked out and saw that they were sliding down a steep, muddy bank into the river. Brake shoes rasped on wheels; then a splash of hooves and a crunching of gravel as the stage began fording the Yellowstone.

It wasn't very deep here but the current was swift. Snows were melting upstream on the Absarokas, in Yellowstone Park. A third of the way across the water was still only hub deep. The bottom was sandy gravel with here and there a loose boulder, "He'll make it all right," Adam Cram predieted, "if he keeps on the right track."

Rolfe felt a sidewise skid of the wheels as the current, pressing like a giant hand, pushed the coach downstream. "Steady, boys!" The driver spoke coaxingly to his four-in-hand and pulled hard on the upstream reins. They were now nearly to midriver. Water crept higher, wetting the coach floor. The girl gathered her skirts and held up her feet a little. The driver shouted a warning. "Look out, folks. If we hit a rock we might tip over. Better unlatch the upstream door, Mr. Cram."

Cram unlatched a door. He and the girl were on the upstream side. The fast brown current was now inches deep in the coach. Again it skidded and skewed, already several lengths too far downstream.

The upstream forward wheel hit a big rock on the river's bottom. It raised the stage on that side and a swift, relentless current did the rest. Rolfe felt himself tipping to a steep angle with the weight of Adam Cram pinioning him. Water surged over him as the angle steepened; then a splashing crash.

The stagecoach tipped completely over, landing on its side three feet deep in water.

"Everybody out!" the driver yelled. "Start wadin' ashore while I cut the traces."

Cram pushed the unlatched door upward and open. "Climb out, Lucia. Quick! Help her, Mr. Rodman."

Rolfe, for the moment submerged and helpless, couldn't see her climb out. The stage was still skidding. He heard snorting horses. A boot kicked his face, although it wasn't intentional. Cram was standing on him to boost the girl upward through the open door.

When Rolfe finally wriggled out from under and got his head above water, he saw that Lucia Ripley was already up through the hole. Cram followed her and then the man who called himself Barry Rodman. The upstream side of the coach was now its roof. Two men and a girl were perched on it while the driver, standing hip-deep in the river, slashed traces to free his teams.

"Are you all right, Mr. Kendall?" It was Lucia calling down through what was now a ceiling trap over Rolfe. The stage was still skidding in short jerks. Rolfe, gasping and spitting water, called back: "Don't worry about me. Just climb on one of those stage horses and ride ashore."

But the stage horses were broken only to harness. "You'll be safer wading, lady," the driver yelled.

When Rolfe at last got up through the trap he saw that Lucia Ripley was neither wading nor riding. She was being carried ashore in the arms of the tall, strong man who'd sat beside her in the coach.

Adam Cram had jumped into the current and was holding tightly to the tail of a horse. The animal was plunging belly-deep toward the north bank. Two other horses were being led by the driver, with the sheepman holding to a tail to keep from being swept off his feet.

The fourth horse, tangled in harness a dozen lengths downriver, was shifting desperately for itself.

Two wheels were above water, one of them smashed beyond repair. As the stage skidded again Rolfe Kendall jumped off into hip-deep water. He began wading ashore, the current battling with his balance at every step.

Ahead of him he saw the tall man whose flat black hat was now floating down, the Yellowstone. He was striding like a sure-footed giant toward the shore. The girl was cradled in his arms and held tightly to his neck. Beyond them stood the cabins and sheds of the Huntley stage station. From them the station master and his hostlers came running; they stood on the bank shouting advice.

The horse whose tail towed Adam Cram was first ashore. Then came the tall man with the girl in his arms. Rolfe, splashing toward them, saw the man set her on her feet. She stood there dripping and bedraggled, her skirts plastered to her legs, her bonnet and combs lost down the river.

Rolfe saw her look up with a smile, weary and grateful. Just as he stumbled ashore he heard her put it into words. "I never would have made it by myself. Thank you so much, Mr. Rodman."

CHAPTER
FOUR

Perry Hamil sat by a hot stove in a cabin back of the Huntley stage house. His shirt and socks hung by the stove, drying. Adam Cram, Rolfe Kendall and a sheepman were sharing the cabin with him; but right now Kendall was sunning himself on a corral fence while the other men were getting warmth from liquor at the station bar. The entire run would be delayed twenty-four hours while the stage company sent out another stage from Billings.

For more reasons than one it suited Hamil. The wrecked coach had been dragged ashore; all baggage, mail and express had been rescued from it. Looking out a window Hamil could see long lines of clothing drying in the sun. Some were party frocks, petticoats and dainty underthings from the baggage of Lucia Ripley. Also everything which had been in Barry Rodman's portmanteau was hanging from a line out there.

Everything but one item, which Hamil had seized upon and brought jealously to this cabin. It was water-soaked but not permanently damaged. Now that he was alone Hamil reopened it cautiously. This was a small, leather-bound family Bible kept for three generations by the Rodmans of Roanoke, Virginia.

Dates of births, marriages and deaths were there. Names of Barry Rodman's parents and grandparents were recorded. Hamil had already memorized every name and date. The entries made it clear that Barry himself had been the last of the Rodmans.

Barry had written his own name on a front flyleaf. It was a distinct round writing with precisely joined letters. Perry Hamil began practicing it at once. The Bozeman lawyers would want him to sign papers. And perhaps they were keeping on file a letter written by Barry Rodman at Roanoke, acknowledging their announcement of his inheritance.

So the delay suited Hamil because it gave him more time to practice the writing; also it gave him an extra day with Adam Cram and the girl. If he could be on a chummy basis with them when they arrived at Bozeman, it would impress the lawyers more than any papers of identification. Those lawyers would meet the stage. How could they doubt him if a leading merchant of the town, backed up by a popular Fort Ellis girl, would personally introduce him? "Barry, shake hands with Wilbur and Ridley Davis."

After that it would be money in the bank. There'd be no room for suspicion or doubt, and therefore no close scrutiny of his writing. He'd be taken for granted. After that he'd spend most of his days at the JR ranch, marking time while they probated the will.

The navy discharge and the three required letters, having been carried in an inner pocket of his jacket, were damp but undamaged.

At supper they were like a family. The spill in a river had broken down all barriers and drawn them together. Adam Cram presided at one end of the table with the Huntley station master at the other. On one side the red-haired army girl sat between Hamil and Kendall. Across from them were the sheepman, the driver and a hostler. The station master's wife waited table.

"The wreck has been reported by telegraph," the station man said. "So your friends at Bozeman know you'll be a day late."

For several years now, as a protection against Indian raids, the various army posts in Montana had been connected by telegraph lines; and the wires were cut in at many of the stage stations along the Yellowstone River.

Adam Cram was in a jolly mood. An afternoon at the station bar had painted wine-red streaks on his face. "Your foreman's goin' to be jealous, Barry," he chuckled, "when he hears about you packing Lucia out of the river. Chances are he'll quit and join the army, where he can keep a closer eye on her."

The effect was to make Lucia turn from Hamil and give her full attention to Rolfe Kendall. "There's no place in the West," she assured him lightly, "where the grass grows greener than it does in the Gallatin Valley."

"Sounds like a right nice range," Rolfe grinned. He remembered his first careless answer to Cram — that his destination was wherever the grass grew greenest.

"Consider Bozeman." Lucia took the tone of a Board of Trade secretary. "Population 1,000, county seat of

Gallatin County; a clear mountain stream teeming with trout, and rising in a chain of lakes twelve miles south, flows through the town. Main Street has four handsome brick blocks, one of which is Mr. Rodman's, seven general stores, one of which is Mr. Cram's, a stone courthouse under construction, three hotels, one bank, one newspaper and a six-company army post only three miles away."

"You forgot to mention eight saloons and a Chinatown alley," Cram added. "Plus three livery barns and a U.S. land office."

Rolfe laughed and made a gesture of capitulation. "You've convinced me. If Barry Rodman'll give me a job punching cows, I'd as lief settle down right there."

"You'll have to see my foreman, Walt Mason," Hamil quipped back.

The same easy banter occupied them till bedtime. When the girl went to her cabin Hamil called after her, "Good night, Lucia."

"Good night, Mr. Rodman."

Hamil grimaced but wasn't discouraged. They still had two days on the road together. He was sure she'd be calling him Barry when they wheeled into Bozeman.

The men's cabin had a cot and two double-deck bunks. Cram and Hamil took the two lowers while Kendall and the driver climbed into uppers. It left the cot unoccupied.

Perry Hamil lay completely relaxed. Every westward mile made his gamble look better. He'd made respectable friends who accepted him as Barry Rodman. Roanoke, Virginia, was a long way from

Bozeman. Not one chance in a thousand there'd be anyone from Roanoke at that far trail's end in Montana. And even if there were they might not have known Barry Rodman. For Rodman had been serving in the navy for a full enlistment period. A sense of confidence and security wrapped Hamil as he fell asleep.

A breakfast gong aroused him. Cram and Kendall were pulling on their boots. The stage driver had been up for an hour tending his horses.

But the cabin's cot, empty at bedtime, now had a sleeper. The man was deep in his blankets, his face buried under an arm and turned toward the wall. "I heard him come in around midnight," Cram said.

The newcomer's boots, jacket and gunbelt were at the foot of his cot. The gun was a frontier model Colt's forty-five. Its scuffed black holster with a hole in the toe seemed vaguely familiar to Hamil.

A worry pricked him and he let the others go out first. Then he leaned over the cot for a closer look. The sleeper stirred slightly, shifted an arm. And Hamil knew him. Here he was again — a shadow from his own past, Harry De Shon of Dodge City, Kansas!

The sense of security deserted Hamil. Had the ex-marshal recognized him, after all, in that Miles City saloon? Was he trailing along to find out why a Texas outlaw named Hamil now called himself Barry Rodman? Two nights ago he'd been run out of Miles City. Was it just an accident that he'd ridden west, the direction taken by Hamil?

Perry Hamil washed and went moodily to breakfast. Two full tables were set. His stagemates, with the exception of Lucia Ripley, were at one of them. Four harnessed horse stood in front with a hostler holding them. "Stage from the west is due any minute," the station master explained.

"Who's our new bunkmate?" Rolfe Kendall asked curiously.

The station master didn't know but the driver did. "He's a guy who killed a man in Miles City about ten hours before we left there. It was self-defense so they couldn't hold him. They just told him to fork his saddle and ride."

"I heard talk about it," Adam Cram remembered. "He used to be a trigger-quick marshal in Kansas. So when they ran him out of Miles City he'd naturally head west."

"Why west?" Hamil questioned.

"Because he's a town tamer by trade. Likely it's the only trade he's got. He'd figure most of the towns that need taming lie west of the divide. Places like Bannack and Virginia City."

"What about Bozeman?" Rolfe suggested.

Cram frowned and shook his head. "With his record, we don't want him in Bozeman. Best job he'd be offered there'd be bouncer at some bar."

Lucia joined them looking fresh and pink. Rolfe Kendall got up to hold a chair for her but Hamil beat him to it. Then the eastbound stage rattled up and five hungry passengers came in to occupy the second table.

They'd boarded at Bozeman and Cram knew them all. "Hello, Cal; hi, Jeb. Hope you don't tip over, fording the river, like we did. Anything new up the line?"

"We ran into a posse at Sweetgrass," Cal said. "They got guns and ropes."

"Who for?"

"Three horse thieves, if they can find 'em. Folks think they're hidin' in the brush along Sweetgrass Creek."

Hamil had studied the schedule. Sweetgrass was the fifth change station west of here.

"How's Bozeman?" Cram prompted. "Still on the boom?"

"About the same," Cal reported. "Chips Charny put in a new bar at the Delmonico. He's fixin' it up right fancy. Claims he'll make it the livest spot in Montana."

"He's got the money to do it," Cram admitted.

"Yeh, Adam, but I don't like the way he made it. He usta run a tradin' post down on the Overland Trail, in Wyoming, and they say he sold whisky to the Sioux; and maybe guns too. The same guns that shot up Custer."

"Maybe the same guns," Cram brooded, "that shot up a stage just three days ago."

"But the government could never prove it," Jeb put in.

"They took away his trader's license."

"Yeh, but for another reason. They canceled his license on account of the way he took advantage of a stranded wagon train, back in '74."

"I heard talk about it," Cram remembered. "Cleaned 'em out of a lot of bounty paper. Soldiers' scrip."

After breakfast everyone went outside to see the eastbound stage off. It had to ford the river and those on the bank watched anxiously. The water level had fallen slightly since yesterday and the crossing was made without mishap.

An hour later they watched another crossing — this time a westbound stage which had left Miles City a full day behind their own. Again the fording was made safely. This coach had breakfasted at Pompey's Pillar so at Huntley it only had to change teams.

Its driver waved derisively as he drove on.

Inside, Hamil found Harry De Shon eating breakfast. The man had strapped on his belt and gun. His eyes met Hamil's briefly, then centered on his food again. *He doesn't remember me. Just the same I hope he doesn't stop at Bozeman.*

Hamil and his fellow passengers got their bags out in front, ready to leave when a relief coach came out from Billings. The driver waited impatiently, his horses harnessed.

But the first to leave was Harry De Shon. They must have passed him during the first night out from Miles City; then the long delay at Huntley had let him catch up. Now he'd be ahead of them again.

As the man put boot to stirrup his eyes once more met Hamil's. This time they lingered with a vague speculation. "Haven't I seen you somewhere before?" the Kansan asked curiously.

47

"Not unless you were in the Navy. That's where I've been the last few years."

De Shon gave a shrug. "My mistake. Didn't mean to be nosy." He stepped into the saddle and jogged on up the Bozeman Trail.

CHAPTER
FIVE

In a little while the relief coach came. The driver hooked up to it and loaded the baggage. Then, twenty-six hours late, Lucia Ripley found herself rolling on toward home.

Army posts had been the only homes she'd ever known. She'd been born on one and throughout childhood had been shifted from fort to fort. She had vivid memories of Fort Leavenworth on the Missouri River; of Fort Fetterman on the Platte, Fort Reno on the Powder, Fort Phil Kearney on the Little Piney, Fort C. F. Smith on the Big Horn. She could remember watching fearfully from stockades as her gallant lieutenant father had ridden out from each of the last four to fight the Indians. Once he'd been brought home with an arrow wound in his cheek. She'd helped her mother put him to bed and had polished the dark red stains from his sabre.

And then these last five years at Fort Ellis, near Bozeman. Except for the reign of terror four years ago, in 1876, they'd been the happiest of her life.

"We'll pass him again." The words came from the man next to her as though he were speaking more to himself than to the others.

"Pass who again?" Lucia asked curiously.

"The man ahead of us."

After a moment's thought she understood. The stage kept going day and night. But a traveler on horseback couldn't do that. He had to sleep and rest his mount.

Lucia looked at Adam Cram. "You said he killed a man at Miles City. Why?"

Cram didn't know. It was the man she knew as Barry Rodman who answered. "To keep from getting killed himself."

The feed merchant pursed his lips, nodding. "It's always been like that, out here. Self-preservation's the first law of the West."

The young man sitting cater-cornered from Lucia said nothing at all. Except that he wore no gun and was uncommonly good-looking, he was much like a hundred other cowboys she'd known. Most of them were drifters, living hand to mouth from one payday to the next. Right now this one had his eyes fixed quizzically on the man facing him; as though something about him needed to be explained.

Lucia herself had noticed a change in him this morning. At supper he'd been relaxed, gay, informal. She remembered his blithe "Good night, Lucia." This morning he seemed alert and tense, like a man on guard.

Rolfe Kendall turned to Cram with a question. "You said something about soldiers' scrip. Do they still give it to soldiers?"

"No," Cram told him. "You don't rate it unless you served in the Mexican War, or in some Indian war before 1854, or are a widow or heir of some soldier who served in those wars. But there's a lot of it still floating around. They call it land warrants, or scrip, or bounty paper. Each eligible applicant gets scrip entitling him or her to 160 acres of public land, providing it's listed at the minimum government price of $1.25 per acre; and most Western public land still is. It makes each piece of 160-acre scrip worth two hundred dollars, if applied on the purchase of public land."

"The scrip's assignable, isn't it?" Lucia asked.

Cram nodded. "Yes, just like a stock certificate. In fact land scrip used to be quoted in the papers on the same page with stock and bond prices. That's what kicked up such a big scandal back in '74, when that crooked trader, Charny, took advantage of a stranded wagon train."

"How did he do it?" Rolfe asked.

"The wagon train started west too late in the season and got caught in deep snow. So it was hung up till spring, camping by Charny's trading post on the Oregon Trail. Twenty wagons and they ran out of grub. To keep from starving they had to buy grub from Charny at his own price. Some of them had bounty paper which they'd planned to buy land with later on. When they ran out of money Charny traded 'em grub for that paper. He kept upping his prices. He made one man pay him scrip good for 160 acres just to get a sack of flour. And on that same day, March 11, 1874, the financial page of the *Denver Times* quoted land scrip at $175. When the government found it out they canceled

Charny's license. So he went to Bozeman and opened a saloon."

At noon they rolled into Billings and stopped to eat. The sheepman quit them and a boot salesman from St. Paul took his place. While they were changing teams the man who'd lost Barry Rodman's hat in the river bought another much like it. Hamil put it on, but his wavy brown hair made him look much more attractive, Lucia thought, when he was bareheaded.

With fresh horses they trotted briskly out of Billings. Ten miles out they passed a horseman heading in the same direction. He was Harry De Shon and he waved a genial hand as the coach swept by him.

Two change stations further on they took supper. It was Stillwater where a new driver came on. "You'll get an all-night boarder, about an hour from now," Cram told the station master. "A town tamer from Kansas named De Shon."

It was still twilight, six miles west of Stillwater, when they met White Calfee's mule train trailing from Bozeman to Miles City. It had five wagons, each with a six-mule team, and a dozen pack animals. Calfee was a man of importance along the Yellowstone and the stage driver rested his team for a minute of talk.

"What about those three horse thieves at Sweetgrass, Mr. Calfee? Did they ketch 'em?"

"Two of 'em. Other one got away."

Adam Cram called through a coach window, "Who you haulin' for this trip, Whitey?"

"Willson and Rich, mostly. I'll bring back hardware for Lamme & Co. Anything down there you want me to pick up?"

"I ordered twenty dozen grain sacks. If it's on the dock, pick it up."

"I'll do that, Adam. Hello there, Lucia. It's good to see you back."

"I got spilled in the river," Lucia laughed, "but Barry Rodman saved me. Mr. Calfee, meet Barry Rodman of Virginia. You knew his Uncle John, of course."

"I sure did." The freighter reached through a stage window to shake hands. "Glad to know you, Barry. Be seein' you around Bozeman."

The mule train moved on east and the stage rumbled on west. Dark came at the next change station. "It's only ninety miles to Bozeman," Cram said.

Rolfe Kendall gave a mock groan. "Ninety more miles! Have a heart, Mr. Cram!"

Lucia looked at him with a provocative smile. "So you're going all the way to Bozeman! When did you decide?"

"About half a minute," Rolfe answered boldly, "after I found out *you* live there."

The cowboy's half-serious tone forced Lucia to make light of it. She turned to the man sitting by her. "Did you hear that, Mr. Barry Rodman? It will be a shame, now, if you don't give him a job on your ranch."

A full moon made bright mellow light. Its beam traced a deep golden path down the river and on the other side the prairie reached north like a silver sea. The trail was smooth here and the driver whipped to a trot. Cigar smoke drifted from the salesman riding on the box. "We oughta make Sweetgrass by midnight," the driver said.

It was exactly midnight when they drew up at the Sweetgrass station. Lucia saw men milling about. Saddle mounts lined the corral fence. Then she remembered talk about a posse chasing horse thieves. At last report two had been caught and a third was still at large.

Was it a sheriff's posse? One look at a huddle of gunslung men told her it wasn't. This was a posse of ranchers and cowboys. She recognized Dale Howard from Shields River and spoke to him. But he pretended not to see her and turned away.

The group stood dourly apart while the stage changed horses. Cram's question, "Where's the sheriff?" drew no response. The two captured thieves weren't in sight. The stage driver asked about the one not yet caught. "We're waitin' fer daylight," a man said, "so we can track him down."

Cram and the driver exchanged uneasy glances. "Let's get going," the merchant fretted.

The stage rolled out at a trot. But at the east edge of town it had to slow down for a ford. Sweetgrass Creek joined the Yellowstone here.

Exactly in the middle of the ford the stage stopped with a jerk. Suddenly Rolfe Kendall leaned across Lucia and pointed out the river-side window. "Look! There's a bull elk swimming the river. What a head! I'd sure like to bag that beauty some cold fall day."

Lucia looked out but couldn't see any swimming elk. She felt a sudden stiffening from the man at her right. Then she heard taut voices from the driver's seat. "Mind if I take a drink, driver? I feel kind of sick."

"Save one for me," the driver said. He lashed his team and the coach splashed on through the ford. When he got to level ruts beyond, he whipped it to a gallop.

But not before Lucia had turned to look beyond Kendall and out the north window. Now she knew why he'd tried to make her look the other way. A lone cottonwood grew near the Sweetgrass ford. Two silhouettes, black against the moonlight, hung from a limb there. The two captured horse thieves. A self-appointed posse had meted out quick punishment.

The girl shuddered. "Thanks," she murmured to Kendall, "for not wanting me to see."

"They oughtn't to do things like that," Kendall said.

Cram mopped beads from his face. "Tomorrow they'll catch the other one," he predicted, "and after that . . ."

"After that, what?" The question came edgily from the man at Lucia's right.

"After that, Barry," Cram finished grimly, "they won't steal any more horses."

No one answered him. The four-in-hand was still at a gallop, the coach swaying like a storm-tossed ship.

After a few minutes of it the driver slowed to a walk. Lucia could hear the horses blowing from the run. Then the boot salesman's shaky voice. "Lucky I bought that pint at Stillwater. I sure needed it."

Then Adam Cram, merchant of Bozeman, took up where he'd left off. "Those men won't steal any more horses — and neither will other men who come along and see them hanging there."

It expressed the cold, ruthless code of the frontier and Lucia knew it was all wrong. She'd always known it was wrong. And she knew that if those men had stolen only money they wouldn't have been lynched. They would have been tried in court and sent to prison. But stealing a saddle horse, here in Montana, could be a capital crime.

"I think lynching," the girl said bitterly, "is the worst crime of all. What do *you* think, Mr. Rodman?"

Before he could answer Adam Cram did it for him, with the air of an oracle. "Look at it this way, Lucia. Suppose one of us was an outlaw. He's been run off his old range and so he moves on to Montana. He rides this stage figuring to settle down at Bozeman or Helena. Then he sees two horse thieves hanging by the road. It'll make him think twice, won't it? He'll say to himself, 'If that's the way they handle outlaws in Montana, I'd better go someplace else.'"

The stage rocked on. After a while it occurred to Lucia that the man beside her had never answered her question. What about the cowboy from Dakota? "What do *you* think, Mr. Kendall?"

"It's an old worn-out case," Rolfe said, "and it goes like this. When you steal a saddle horse you leave its owner afoot. Afoot the owner might die of thirst while walking on across a desert. That makes it murder. So you lynch the horse thief as a guy who might have committed murder. In this deal there's no-desert; nobody'll thirst to death on the bank of the Yellowstone River. So the whole case is wrong; it's rotten wrong."

His stock went up with Lucia. He was forthright — a man with straight clear thoughts who didn't hide them. No mystery about him, as there was about Barry Rodman.

From the first Lucia had sensed an elusive mystery about the tall, brown-eyed man at her right. It was a mystery which compelled her interest and to pierce it she kept prompting him. "You haven't taken sides yet, Mr. Rodman. Do you agree with Mr. Cram, or with me and Rolfe Kendall?"

To her surprise he met her eyes with a frank smile. His answer came in a soft Southern accent. "If you'll stop calling me Mr. Rodman, I'll tell you."

"Very well, Barry. Tell us what you think."

"I think Mr. Cram's right on one count; if I was a horse thief I'd be scared stiff and I'd get fast out of Montana. But Kendall's right too. Lynching's wrong; it's stupid and rotten wrong."

They changed horses at Big Timber where the boot salesman refilled his flask. Then they rattled on up the starlit trail. Adam Cram slept. But for Lucia the shock at Sweetgrass had made sleep impossible. The man at her right sat with closed eyes but she sensed he was awake; as tensely awake as herself. The boot salesman was awake because she heard him share his flask with the driver.

Kendall too kept drowsily awake. Day was breaking when he looked from his window. "What do they call that high mountain?"

"It's Crazy Peak," Lucia told him. The peak had a cap of snow and reared about twenty miles to the north; it was the first high, timbered mountain they'd sighted.

"Looks like a right lonesome range," Rolfe said. "If I was that third horse thief — the one they haven't caught yet — it's right where I'd head for."

She wondered if he shared her own half-guilty thought about that uncaught thief. Ever since the sight of those lynchings at Sweetgrass, she'd been hoping he'd get away.

The light broadened although it wasn't yet sunup. Cram still slept. Ten miles beyond Big Timber they slowed to a creep in order to cross a sharp gully which rains had cut across the trail.

A man with a level rifle arose from that gully. Lucia saw him and heard his voice. "Hands up, driver! I won't hurt anybody if you do like I say. Everybody out with his hands high."

The man was young, haggard, disheveled and desperate. Lucia heard the driver's thick voice. "You can't get away with this." But since he didn't shoot he must have already raised his hands. His voice had whisky in it; the salesman had been too generous with his flask.

Kendall asked in a whisper, "Are you armed, Rodman?"

"No."

"Neither am I. So it's his drop. Wake up, Mr. Cram."

The holdup man wasn't masked. To Lucia he seemed hardly more than a boy. A pallor of panic on his face could mean that he knew what had happened at Sweetgrass Creek. He kept his aim mainly on the driver. "I'm not after money," he said. "You got just two things I want. I want one horse and one saddle. I can see a saddle in the backside baggage rack."

Lucia caught a whisper from Rolfe Kendall. "He's the third thief, all right. Likely his mount played out or got shot." Raising his voice Rolfe called through a window. "We got a lady in here, mister."

"She won't get hurt," the rifleman promised. "Let her stay right there, if she wants. Rest of you pile out."

The driver and the salesman were already on the ground. The three men passengers got out to join them, Adam Cram's face gray with fright. The young outlaw had already taken the driver's gun.

"Damn this run!" Lucia heard him complain. "If it ain't Injuns, it's somethin' else. It's your play, mister. Which horse do you want?"

"Which one's broken to saddle?" the rifleman demanded. "Don't try to fool me. If you pick the wrong one, I'll shoot."

"The off-lead bronc's been rid," the driver said.

"Take him out of harness. Then grab that saddle off the back rack. Saddle him up. Rest of you lie face down right over there."

Looking from the coach, Lucia saw the men passengers flatten themselves by the trail. The outlaw swung his aim back to the driver. A jingle of chains from up front meant that one of the stage horses was being untraced.

Then the driver went sullenly to a rack at the rear and from it took Rolfe Kendall's saddle.

"Toss it on," the holdup man commanded.

The movement of a hand caught Lucia's eye. It was the outstretched hand of Rolfe Kendall as he lay face down beside three other men. Of the four, Rolfe was nearest the horse on which the driver was now cinching a saddle.

Lucia saw Rolfe's hand close on an egg-size stone.

Her impulse was to cry out and beg him not to resist. With only a stone he couldn't win against a repeating rifle.

"Now hit the dirt yourself," the rifleman said to the driver when the cinch was tight. He punched the man with the bore of his weapon.

The driver dropped face down beside Cram. Lucia kept her eyes in a terrified fascination on Kendall's right hand. Just as the outlaw put foot to stirrup, she saw Rolfe jump up and throw the stone. He threw it not at the man but at the horse. Stung by the stone, the horse jumped sideways. The man in the act of mounting was thrown off balance and his leg swing missed the saddle.

The stage horse, only half broken to saddle, kept jumping and it made the outlaw hit the ground. He landed on his feet with the rifle still in his hand. Rolfe Kendall was lunging headfirst at his stomach. Lucia half screamed, expecting a shot at point-blank range.

Instead of shooting the rifle, the outlaw clubbed it and crashed its barrel on Rolfe's head. Both men went down, Rolfe from the blow on his head, the outlaw from the impact of a lunge into his stomach. "Help him!" Lucia cried out to four prone men. One of them got to his knees. Then the outlaw jumped to his feet and clicked his rifle to a cock. "Keep down, you guys!" He fired and sent a bullet through a flat black hat.

Rolfe Kendall lay motionless on the ground and Lucia saw blood at his head. The man who'd clubbed him down jumped into a saddle. He made off at a hard run, north toward a high, timbered mountain.

CHAPTER
SIX

He was out of sight by the time they brought Rolfe to his senses. "It's only a bump on the noggin," the driver said. Sobered by the holdup, he bathed the wound with water from the river and brought an aid kit from the box. The blow had cut a bloody gash and Lucia Ripley, kneeling in the dusty trail rut, taped it carefully. "Quit making a fuss," Rolfe said. He got up and went to the coach. "It's breakfast time and I'm hungry."

It was only four miles to Gage's ranch and they made it at a walk, using only a two-horse team. By the time they reached Gage's, Cram was orating again. "Round up some men and guns!" he shouted to the station master.

After reporting the holdup Cram mopped his wide, red face and turned to Lucia. "We can telegraph that posse at Sweetgrass and they'll track him to Crazy Mountain. I sure hope they catch him."

"I don't," Lucia said.

"Neither do I," echoed Rolfe Kendall. "He looked to me like just a scared kid — about ten times scareder 'n we were."

Lucia looked at him askance. "If you didn't want him to get away, why did you throw that stone?"

"Who said anything about not wanting him to get away? I said I hope the Sweetgrass lynchers don't catch him."

The army girl nodded. There was a big difference.

"The only safe place for that boy," Rolfe went on, "is the jail at Bozeman. The worst he'd get from a court would be two to five years. But if those Sweetgrassers catch him . . ."

"He'd be a goner," the man across from him broke in. "So you threw the stone to save his neck. You think they'll catch him?"

"Odds are against him," Rolfe said. "He daren't show up at a ranch or settlement. Hell have to hide in the timber without any grub, with forty men beating around for him."

"Sorry I let you down, Kendall."

"But you didn't, Barry." Lucia gave him an approving smile. At her cry "Help him," only one of four prone men had started to get up. Lucia looked at the new hat he'd bought at Billings and saw proof of it. A bullet had passed cleanly through the crown.

Perry Hamil, eating breakfast at Gage's, heard the click of a telegraph key. This was another of the Yellowstone River stage stations where the wire joining army posts had been cut in, so that Indian forays could be speedily reported.

This time it was a commercial call from Bozeman. The station man relayed it to the breakfasters. "The Bozeman paper wanted to know about that spill at Huntley. While I had 'em on the line, I told 'em about the holdup this morning. They said Sheriff McKinzie's already heading this way."

Lucia looked from Rolfe Kendall to Perry Hamil. "It will be all over town by the time we get there. You'll be heroes, both of you."

A smile dried on Hamil's lips. Publicity like that could be a little more than he'd bargained for. He wanted to arrive as Barry Rodman, vouched for by his fellow-passengers. But anything more than that could spell trouble. A large curious crowd meeting the stage might have one ex-Texan in it. And one, if he'd come recently from the El Paso district, could be enough to scuttle Hamil.

His nerves were on edge as the stage left Gage's. A stop three miles further on was merely to throw off a mail pouch at Hunter's Hot Springs. Beyond Hunter's they caught up with a bull train plodding west. There were ten wagons, each with eight yoke; one hundred and sixty oxen in all. Store goods for the merchants at Bozeman.

They passed the mouth of Shields River, coming in from the north. "An historic spot," Lucia said, "because John Bozeman and Jim Bridger separated right here."

"You mean the famous scouts?" Rolfe asked her.

The girl nodded. "Each of them blazed a trail from the Platte, in Wyoming, to Bozeman and the Virginia City gold fields. Bozeman came north along the east side of the Big Horns and Bridger came up the west side. Their trails met on the Yellowstone; then they came together up the river just this far."

"And then?"

"They disagreed about how to get over those mountains." Lucia pointed to a high range directly west. "Jim Bridger wanted to go up Shields River, then up Brackett Creek to cross the divide at what we now call Bridger Pass. John Bozeman wanted to go the way this stage will go, over Bozeman Pass. Each scout went his own way and Bozeman's turned out to be quickest and shortest."

In midmorning the stage made Benson's Landing and stopped at Burns' store there. A half dozen flat-bottom mackinaws were moored at a boat landing. "When the water's right," Cram explained to Hamil, "freight can go down the Yellowstone by boat; but it generally has to come upriver by bull or mule train."

A big florid man came out of the store. He wore a gray cattleman's hat and his voice boomed. "Is Barry Rodman on this stage?"

"You bet he is," Cram said. "Barry, meet Mike Lockhart of the Circle X. He'll be a neighbor of yours up Middle Fork of the Gallatin."

Lockhart's grip, meant to be hearty, was like a vise and it hurt a little. The man was six feet six and wide as a door. His eyes gave Hamil a shrewd appraisal. "You don't look much like a tenderfoot, young fella."

Cram chuckled. "If he was yesterday, he's not today." He thumbed toward a hole through Hamil's hat. "He's already been shot at."

Mike Lockhart ignored the others and spoke bluntly to Hamil. "They told me you were on this stage, so I rode over the hill to see you. Had to ride this way anyway, to look for some summer grass."

"What," Hamil asked cautiously, "do you want to see me about?"

"I'm a man of few words," Lockhart said. "My land is in two parcels with yours in between. So I need your place to square out my own. Just before he died I offered your uncle a flat sum for every hoof and acre of the JR. Sixty thousand dollars. The offer still stands. Spot cash. Think it over. Stock raising's a risky business. An Easterner like you, without any experience, could lose his shirt."

Hamil's pulse quickened. This was exactly what he wanted. A fast turn for cash and then a fast ride out of Montana.

Then he bit his lip. The estate had to go through probate first. "It's not mine to sell yet, Mr. Lockhart. But the offer sounds fair and I'll certainly think it over."

"Do that. And remember this. The JR's worth more to me than it is to anyone else." The big cattleman went to a hitchrack and climbed a horse. Hamil watched him ride off upriver.

With fresh teams and a new driver, the stagecoach left the river and moved upgrade toward a pass. Halfway up they changed teams at Hopper's and had lunch there. An hour beyond Hopper's they topped the divide and looked down on the vast lush valley of the Gallatin.

Hamil spoke to Lucia Ripley. "You say John Bozeman came this way. And after that, I suppose, a lot of trail herds began coming up from Texas."

"Yes," she said. "Nelson Story brought the first herd up from Texas, in 1866. He settled in Bozeman and still lives there."

66

It didn't greatly disturb Hamil. In 1866 he himself had been only twelve years old. There was always a chance that a few cowboys of those early trail days had also taken root in Bozeman. There were many risks, but this play was for big stakes. A chip worth sixty thousand had already been tossed into the pot.

Ten Mile House, just west of the pass, was the last change station. From there four fresh horses could trot nearly all the way to Bozeman. Just short of the town they stopped at the gate of a military stockade.

"Dad!" Lucia Ripley jumped out into the arms of a cavalry captain. A bevy of army women were there, too, to welcome her.

Amid a chatter of greetings her baggage was unloaded. A minute later Lucia was waving goodbye to her stagemates.

The coach rattled on and in ten more minutes was raising dust in Main Street at Bozeman.

It wasn't the shabby frontier town that Hamil had more or less expected. The hotel they stopped at was a three-story brick; several other brick blocks were in sight. He wondered which was his own. Everything else was frame but there were no false fronts like the ones at Miles City. Carriages and buggies rolling by had well-dressed people in them. Every hitchrack was full; and the board walks, raised a foot above the dust level, were wide and milling with shoppers.

Hamil saw a sprinkling of cowboys, soldiers, Indians. Across the street a covered wagon was drawn up, its family of immigrants gazing curiously at the stage. The store beyond it had a fresh-painted front. In all the town looked clean and prosperous.

Perry Hamil stepped out on the walk and there, waiting cordially, were two who could only be Davis & Davis, attorneys for the estate of John Rodman.

It wasn't even necessary for Adam Cram to do the honors. "You're Barry, of course." One of the lawyers looked knowingly at the hole in Hamil's hat. "Well, well! So you finally got here. I'm Ridley Davis and this is my brother Wilbur."

Cram edged in. "He almost didn't make it, Wilbur. Two stages earlier and he'd've been scalped by Indians. You heard about the upset we had at Huntley?"

"Yes, and about the holdup." Wilbur Davis gave his client a clap on the shoulder. "We hear you carried a fair lady from the river. Your uncle would have been proud of you. Is that your portmanteau on top? Boy, take it up to Room 216."

At least forty people stood close by, giving curious inspection to John Rodman's heir. A few who'd been cronies of John Rodman came up to shake hands. In a moment an informal reception was being held on the walk. Adam Cram made the introductions. "Barry, meet Doctor Osborne. And this is your banker, General Willson; and Charley Rich; and Frank Harper, our leading blacksmith; and my competitor in the feed business, Mr. Tracy; and Hank Galen who owns the stage line . . ."

Hamil looked for Rolfe Kendall but the cowboy had disappeared in the crowd. A reporter for the *Courier* came up. "What are your plans, Mr. Rodman? May we say you expect to make Bozeman your permanent home?"

Hamil smiled wearily. "Please, I'm a little bushed, right now."

"Of course he is," echoed Ridley Davis. He was shorter and a bit plumper than his brother. "Who wouldn't be, after three hundred miles on that stage?"

He took his client's arm and got him into the hotel's lobby. The host, Phil Skehan, was waiting for them. "This is an occasion, gentlemen. Step into the bar and have one on the house."

"Just what I need," Perry Hamil said gratefully. With the lawyers he followed Skehan into the bar.

After one drink the lawyers themselves stood treat. Then Adam Cram came in and paid for another one. It was during this third round that Hamil remembered certain credentials in his inside pocket.

He brought out an unsealed envelope and handed it to Ridley Davis. "Better take these off my hands before I lose them. They got wet in the river."

The lawyers took a look, saw a discharge from the navy and three letters. One was a letter he himself had written to Barry Rodman.

"Just a formality," he murmured in a tone of apology.

"Stop in at our office tomorrow, Barry," his brother suggested, "and we'll brief you on the estate."

Presently they were gone and Manager Skehan conducted Hamil up to Room 216. It was a big room cornering on Main and Bozeman streets. Across the side street Hamil saw a frame bank and across Main a new two-story brick whose cornice had RODMAN

BLOCK on it. A mellow glow filled Hamil. That was a blue chip in the jackpot he'd gambled for. And the game was moving along smoothly. Not a breath of suspicion. What boobs they were, these Bozemanites! Hamil lighted a cigaret, kicked off his boots. He sat staring across at the Rodman Block. And how much had that cattleman offered him for the ranch? Sixty thousand spot cash! The man from El Paso blew cool smoke rings and a smile of assurance settled smugly on his face.

Then came a tap at his door. Hamil got lazily to his sock feet and moved toward it. A boy with ice water, maybe, or a maid with fresh towels.

When he opened the door, Manager Skehan himself stood there with a letter. "It just came in, Mr. Rodman."

"Thanks." Perry Hamil took it and closed the door.

His brow clouded when'he saw the postmarks. It had been mailed at Roanoke, Virginia, and had arrived at the Bozeman post office only an hour ago.

Had it come on his own stage? Probably not. His stage had been delayed twenty-six hours at Huntley; during the delay it had been overtaken and passed by a coach which had left Miles City a day later than his own. So this letter could have been posted at Roanoke a full day after the departure of Barry Rodman.

It was the handwriting which most disturbed Hamil. This was a girl's writing! A girl so close to Barry Rodman that she'd written him less than twenty-four hours after he'd said goodbye.

70

A terrifying possibility hit Hamil. He hadn't calculated on Barry Rodman's being entangled with a woman. As a boy in the navy he'd naturally have a girl or two. But suppose it had gone farther than that. For all Hamil knew, Barry Rodman might even have been married!

Hamil stared bleakly at the envelope. If there was a Mrs. Barry Rodman his whole venture was washed up. He could fool Barry's lawyers but he couldn't fool his widow.

With a sense of disaster Hamil slit the envelope open. His eyes fixed with dismay on the salutation. "My dearest one." Would anyone but a wife call him that?

It was a long letter and Perry Hamil couldn't wait to know the worst. He skipped to the end and read:

. . . till the day when you send for me, and loving you every minute, your
DEVOTED WIFE-TO-BE, DIANE

So there'd been no marriage. But Hamil could take small comfort from it. A fiancée was hardly less dangerous than a wife. She had a ring on her finger and expected to be sent for. There'd be a stream of letters from her and they couldn't be answered. She'd know in a minute if Hamil tried to fake an answer. He'd use the wrong words and the wrong writing. He didn't even know her last name or the street number of her house.

He was licked and Perry Hamil admitted it with a gambler's shrug. The best he could do would be to talk the lawyers out of a small advance. Maybe a thousand dollars for expense money. Then he'd toss in his hand. He'd saddle up one of the JR horses to ride fast and far from Montana.

CHAPTER
SEVEN

Hamil rang a bell and had supper sent up to his room. He wanted to be alone and think.

The stake was small now but he might as well rake in what he could. He might send Diane a telegram. "Arrived safely. Love. Barry." That would stall her off for a few days while he coaxed an advance from the lawyers. Handwriting wouldn't show in a telegram.

But blast it! he didn't know the girl's last name. Hamil sifted through the portmanteau to find a record of it. There were a few letters written to Barry Rodman in the navy — but the only name signed was Diane. So he couldn't even address her by wire.

In the morning Davis & Davis might ask him to sign a few papers. So Perry Hamil practiced for an hour. Over and over he copied the signature "Barry Rodman."

Pulling the wool over the lawyers' eyes wouldn't be too hard. And the Roanoke girl wouldn't begin to be suspicious for a week or two yet. Barry had probably written her from Miles City, describing his steamboat ride up the river.

Why hadn't he married her in Roanoke and brought her along to Montana? To find out Hamil read the girl's long letter from beginning to end. Her parents, he learned, had insisted that she finish school first. She was enrolled in a young ladies' college at Richmond and had one more year there. After graduation she'd come west to marry Barry Rodman at Bozeman.

That was the plan they'd settled on. A wedding in June a year from now. Except for one hitch, it gave Hamil all the time he needed. By then he'd have his hands on the estate. The hitch was a girl who'd insist on finding out why he didn't answer her letters.

One other bit of information in today's letter struck Hamil as important. He read it again.

... It was so thoughtful of your Uncle John to make you a present of a year's subscription to the Bozeman weekly. It still has a few months to run and it's being delivered at my house now. You may be sure I'll read every issue to learn all I can about that new world of the West which is yours, and which some day will be mine too.

The Bozeman newspaper! So the girl in Virginia would be reading it every week! Perhaps the current issue was already in the mails, on its way to Roanoke by stage, steamboat and train.

What would it say about Barry Rodman?

Hamil put on his boots and went down to the lobby. There he bought the latest *Avant Courier* and saw two front page headlines. One story about the stage tipping over in the Huntley ford; the other about a holdup by a fugitive horse thief.

74

Both stories featured the name of Barry Rodman. One told about Barry and a popular army girl who'd ridden three hundred miles on a stage together; how at the river upset he'd carried her safely ashore. The editor, to squeeze the last drop of news value out of it, had given the incident a tinge of romance.

The germ of a thought came to Hamil. He put the paper in his pocket and crossed to Sackett's saloon. It was an orderly place without games or entertainers. A pair of bull-whackers stood at the bar with beers. The bartender seemed to know Hamil by sight. "Good evening, Mr. Rodman. What'll it be?" He'd probably seen the sidewalk reception at the stage's arrival.

Hamil ordered a highball, preoccupied with his new angle of thought. The Roanoke girl would read the Bozeman paper. From it she'd learn of Barry Rodman's safe arrival. She'd learn too that he'd rescued a beautiful redhead from the river.

What would Diane of Roanoke think about that? Nothing, at first. But suppose the days went by and no answers came to her letters! Suppose as time went on she read other items coupling Lucia Ripley with Barry Rodman! What would she think then?

She was a Virginia girl with a natural pride and restraint — the kind who wouldn't keep clinging to a man who'd clearly become interested elsewhere. It would need a bit of scheming and Perry Hamil, sipping his highball at Sackett's bar, began the scheming at once. He took the local paper from his pocket and opened it to the social column. There was to be an auction box supper next week at Chestnut Hall. The ladies would bring baskets and the men would bid for them, the high bidder in each case taking the lady across to supper at the Laclede. Results would be published, because all proceeds would go to the new hospital fund.

So his next step was clear to Perry Hamil. He must bid in Lucia Ripley's basket and the more he paid for it, the better.

Let the Roanoke girl read about it and draw her own conclusions.

Hamil couldn't write her. But he could give her the silent treatment and let news stories do the rest. In time she'd consider herself jilted and drop quietly from Barry Rodman's life.

"Seein' as you're gonna be my new landlord," the bartender said, "have another on the house."

Hamil missed his meaning until he remembered that this saloon was one of several shops on the ground floor of the Rodman Block.

A clink of spurs drew his attention to a cowboy coming in from the street. The man was young and had solid, ruddy good looks. Dusty *chaparajos* and a holstered gun meant he'd just ridden in from the range.

The man stopped a pace just short of the bar to ask a question. "I'm looking for Roy Hickey or Dutch Yeager. Either of 'em been in here?"

"They were in right after supper," the barman said. "But they didn't stay long."

"Thanks. I'll try Jake's Place." The man turned away but before he got to the door the saloonman called him back.

"Hold on a minute, Walt. Long as you're here you might as well meet your new boss. Mr. Rodman, shake hands with your foreman, Walt Mason."

Walt Mason's tanned face had a smile of welcome as he came back to the bar. He was about Hamil's age and height, clean-shaven, with a firm mouth and straight-looking blue eyes. "We've been expectin' you. Sorry I couldn't meet your stage. When are you goin' out to the ranch?"

"In a day or two," Hamil said. He could feel strength and capability in the grip of Mason's hand.

"Whenever you feel like it, just go out there and make yourself at home, Mr. Rodman."

"You make me feel old, Walt. Call me Barry. I heard talk about you on the stage and they said you were on roundup."

The foreman's face became suddenly serious, almost grim. "I was. But somethin' came up that needs tendin' to right here in Bozeman. If you'll excuse me I'll get busy on it now." Again Walt Mason started toward the door and again an afterthought turned him back. "Hold on a minute. You're the boss. So I reckon you ought to know about it. Want to come along?"

Hamil didn't. This was probably some minor ranch complication and he didn't want to be bothered with it. At the same time he wanted Mason's confidence and respect. The foreman's acceptance of him as Barry Rodman, in the days to come, could be a big asset.

"Sure I do." Hamil joined Walt Mason at the door. "What's it all about?"

As they walked half a block west to Jake's Place, Walt explained why he'd come to town. "In March I spotted a rincon of grass up near Butte Meadows, at the top of Squaw Creek. Nothing was feeding on it and it was going to waste. I figured it was just about big enough for a hundred head. So I told two of my hands to shove a hundred steers up there."

"Did they?"

"They said they did, and I took their word for it. In May they quit and came to town. And this morning a roundup crew rode up to that rincon to bring down those hundred steers. But the steers weren't there. They hadn't been there. The rincon grass was still high and untrampled." The grim look came again to Mason's face as he pushed through the swinging half-doors at Jake's Place. "Seen Roy Hickey or Dutch Yeager?" he asked Jake.

"Not tonight, Walt."

Mason tried the Delmonico next. The pair he was looking for weren't there. Hamil's glimpse of the place reminded him of gossip from a muleteer on the stage road. About an ex-trader named Chips Charny who boasted that he'd make this bar the fanciest in Montana. It already sparkled with gilt and glitter. A dazzling blond hostess was busy fascinating the more prosperous of the customers. Three other bar girls were in sight, two of them dancing with soldiers from the fort, another one coaxing a customer to a faro bank. On a deep-end stage, piano and violin music jangled with a discord of talk, laughter and song.

78

A short, broad man in a cutaway coat stood with his back to the bar. He had thin, oily hair plastered to his scalp, curved and waxy mustaches, and a big diamond in his tie. Hamil tagged him at once as Chips Charny, who'd made his first stake on the Overland Trail selling whisky and guns to the Sioux.

"Have one on me, Walt," Charny invited. "You and your friend both."

The JR man gave an abrupt "No thanks" and left the place. Hamil followed him down the walk. "I don't cotton to that guy, Barry. Kinda gives me the creeps. Let's try the Palace."

From the Palace they moved on to the Tivoli Beer Hall. Hickey and Yeager were at neither place.

"They were in here last night," the Tivoli man said. "Yeager was flashing a roll. Must've cleaned up in a crap game somewhere."

As they went out Mason gave a cryptic nod. "Maybe he did. Or maybe he drove a hundred steers down into Idaho and sold 'em."

"How much would they bring?"

"About four thousand at an honest market. About half that much at a rustlers' market. Let's take a look in here."

They turned in at a hotel bar. It was a frame hotel called the Northern Pacific. The only customer there was a cowboy with a holstered gun at his hip.

He grinned and waved a hand. "Hi, Barry. I thought you'd be in bed by this time, after a seventy-hour stage ride."

Hamil was glad to see him. Rolfe Kendall calling him Barry made just one more voucher. "Walt, meet Rolfe Kendall from Dakota. He's a cattle handler by trade. Rolfe, this is the JR foreman Lucia was telling us about." The gun, Hamil guessed, had been in Kendall's baggage roll during the stage ride from Miles City.

Mason and Kendall exchanged quick appraisals and each seemed to approve of the other. Kendall spoke first. "Which reminds me, Barry. Lucia said maybe I could get a saddle job at the JR. And you said it'd be up to your foreman."

Hamil looked at Walt Mason. "How about it? Do we have an opening?"

"We've been short-handed," Mason admitted, "ever since Hickey and Yeager quit us in May. If you like, Kendall, I could take you on right now."

"Consider me hired." Rolfe plumped his beer glass on the bar. "When and where do I start?"

"Come along with us," Mason said, "and start right now."

On the way to the next bar he explained to Kendall about a hundred missing steers. "So the next chore," the foreman finished with a snap. "is to find those guys and make 'em talk."

Half an hour later they'd canvassed the eighth and last saloon without finding their men.

Mason had a baffled look but Rolfe came up with a shrewd suggestion. "Why not check the livery barns? If they've got broncs in one of them, they're still in town."

Bozeman had three livery stables, two on Main and one on a side street. It was at Fridley's barn, on a side street, that they found saddle mounts belonging to Hickey and Yeager.

"They won't be callin' for 'em till morning," Walt said, "so we might as well turn in."

But again Rolfe Kendall had a thought. "Look, fellas. You asked for 'em at eight bars. Maybe they stopped in at one of 'em since you were there. In that case they know you're hunting for them; which would make 'em grab their horses and hightail out of town."

Walt gave him a keen look. "That's using your head, Kendall. If they've got a guilty conscience, and someone tips them I came in from the roundup to look for 'em, they'll want to ride fast outa town. So let's stay right here, for a while, and wait for 'em."

A rafter lantern dimly lighted the stable aisle. Stalls on either side each had a haltered horse. At the back an open door, wagon-wide, gave to a cinder-paved alley. A harness room was to the right of the alley door.

The barn's night man looked curiously at Walt Mason, "Whatcha want with those guys, Walt? They don't ride for you any more, do they?"

"Not any more. Look, Bud. Go to the front office and don't tell anybody we're here. We'll wait in the harness room. If Hickey and Yeager show up, let them pay their stable bill. Stay right there when they come back to saddle up."

"Anything you say, Walt." The night man returned to his magazine in the front office.

Hamil followed Mason and Kendall into the harness room. Of the three, only Hamil was unarmed. He must stay unarmed, too. A gun at his hip would put him out of character. He was Barry Rodman of Virginia and he mustn't forget it.

Kendall held a match to Mason's cigaret, "How do you want to handle 'em?"

"I'll just ask 'em a few simple questions," Walt said tersely.

They wouldn't admit anything, Hamil thought. This was June, and the hundred missing steers were last seen in March. Why should Hickey and Yeager admit anything now?

Three cigarets later Hamil heard someone coming down the barn aisle. Mason peered out. "It's Hickey," he whispered. "Yeager's not with him. Let's see if he saddles both horses."

Hamil nodded. Yeager could be waiting at some bar or rooming house while Hickey brought both the mounts. By following Hickey, Mason would be able to confront both men.

Again the foreman peered out. His next report was: "He's just taking his own horse; so I'd better stop him."

He walked out into the barn aisle with Hamil and Kendall at his heels. A man had saddled a horse and was in the act of tying a blanket roll behind the cantle. In the dimness Hamil could see only that he was a long, lean man with a holstered gun.

"Figurin' to leave town, Hickey?" The challenge from Mason made the man spin about, his hand whipping to the butt of his gun.

"I wouldn't do that," Walt Mason warned.

Hickey's eyes jerked from one to another of three men. His hand dropped to his side. "Where's Yeager?" Mason demanded.

"Dutch? I ain't seen him tonight."

"You're lying, Hickey. You and Yeager had a drink together at Sackett's bar. Where did Dutch get that roll he flashed at the Tivoli?"

"He diced for it. Any law against that? See here, Mason. We don't ride for you any more. What Dutch and me do is none of your business."

"What you did with those steers, back in March, is my business. Come clean, Hickey. What *did* you do with 'em?"

"We left 'em in that grass patch up Squaw Crik, like you wanted."

"That grass patch is still fresh. No cattle sign anywhere on it. Look, Hickey. You're going to tell me the truth if I have to beat it out of your hide."

"You're gangin' me. You're three to one." Hickey looked sullenly toward Hamil and Kendall, who'd stopped a few paces farther back in the aisle.

"We're one to one. Just you and me." Walt Mason snatched the gun from Hickey's holster and tossed it aside. Then he drew his own gun. "Hold this, Barry, while I knock the truth out of this bozo." He tossed his forty-five to Hamil.

"You fellas keep out of this," Mason said over his shoulder. To Roy Hickey he promised: "I guarantee they won't touch you. But I will. I'll touch you up good. Like this." He slapped Hickey hard on the jaw.

Hickey's swing missed. Hamil, watching, saw that he was no match for Mason. The JR foreman let loose a volley of jabs and punches. He slapped the man with his right, backhanded him with his left. Hickey after a few awkward swings staggered back, both hands over his face. Mason had no mercy for him. He closed in, his knuckles cutting the man's eyebrow and drawing blood from his lip.

Hickey cowered. "Stop it!" he begged.

"Soon as you tell me the truth," Mason agreed. His next punch dropped Hickey flat in the stable aisle.

The JR foreman took him by the collar, jerked him upright. Holding him at arm's length he hammered a drumbeat of blows to mouth, cheek, nose. "Any time you want me to stop, just say what you did with those steers."

Hickey's face was cut to ribbons before he gave up. He sank to his knees, arms about Mason's legs. "Stop!" he pleaded. "I'll tell you."

"Let's have it," Mason said. "And if you don't convince me I'll start on you again."

The eyes that looked up at him were bleary with tears and blood. "We drove 'em up Swan Crik, 'stead of up Squaw Crik, and left 'em in Hyalite Park."

"Who with?"

"With nobody. We just left 'em in Hyalite Park and rode back to the ranch."

"Somebody picked 'em up in the park later, huh, and drove 'em to Idaho. Who was it?"

"I don't know."

Mason slapped him again, shook him. "You've got a few teeth I haven't knocked out yet. Talk straight."

"A man met us on the trail," Hickey whimpered. "He gave Dutch a wad of money and whispered something. I don't know what he said. The man had a patch over his eye and looked like he was part Indian. He rode off and I never saw him again."

"Go on."

"Dutch said it was money the man owed him. He said the man gave him a message from you. We was to take the bunch up Swan Crik, 'stead of up Squaw. That's all I know, honest to God it is."

A sharp command popped from the alley doorway. "Reach high, everybody!"

Hamil turned and saw a man framed against the night light. He was a thick-set man with a gun in each hand. One gun was aimed at Walt Mason's back; the other covered Rolfe Kendall.

It was a complete drop and not to be defied. Mason's hands went slowly up. He was unarmed, having tossed his gun to Perry Hamil. Rolfe, standing at Hamil's elbow, also raised his hands.

Hamil had dropped Mason's gun in a side pocket of his coat. He wore no gunbelt or holster, and in the dimness didn't seem to be armed. To Dutch Yeager he must have looked less dangerous than the others.

"You got too big a mouth, Hickey." The gun in Yeager's left hand roared and its bullet drilled Hickey through the breast.

"Shows you I mean business," the man warned. "You other guys better keep your hands up or you'll get the same dose. Hey, you in the flat hat. Lead that saddled horse out here in the alley. Then I'll blow town."

Hamil had raised his hands shoulder high. He looked at Dutch Yeager and knew him for a killer. Perry Hamil, for years the most feared outlaw on the lower Rio Grande, was a killer himself. He knew the mind of killers and so he knew what this one would do if and when a saddled horse was led to the alley.

The man had just killed Hickey in front of three witnesses. He'd hardly ride away and leave those three to tell tales in court. They were at his mercy; their hands were up and he had two guns. Three bullets and there'd be no tales told.

With that stab of thought, Hamil forgot he was Barry Rodman. He was Perry Hamil and could draw with the speed of light.

His right hand flashed to his coat pocket and came out with Walt Mason's gun. Its roar brought a scream from Yeager. Yeager went to his knees shooting, but shooting wild. Another shot came from Rolfe Kendall who jumped into the fight with his own gun.

Yeager hit the alley cinders, his face contorted from the agony of a broken arm. Hamil's bullet had cut the bone between elbow and shoulder.

In ten jumps Walt Mason was there and picked up the man's guns. He looked curiously from Kendall to Hamil. "That was a big chance you fellows took, him with a two-gun drop. He was only hit once. Which one of you guys nailed him?"

"Not me," Hamil said quickly. "I missed him a mile." That was his story and he must stick to it. A fast draw, and pinpoint shooting, didn't match the character of Barry Rodman.

Mason's back had been toward them. But not Kendall's. Rolfe fixed an odd stare on Hamil. "Are you sure you missed him, Barry?"

"Of course I did. I don't know beans about guns. It was you who downed him."

"Was it?" A speculative smile on Rolfe Kendall's lips brought a sting of worry to Perry Hamil. He and Kendall alone knew whose bullet had downed Dutch Yeager.

CHAPTER
EIGHT

Hamil slept till noon. When he went down to the Laclede's dining room a friendly, personable man in a frock coat was waiting for him. "I'm Alderson of the *Avant Courier*." The newspaper man sat opposite Hamil and ordered coffee. "I suppose you realize you're front page news, young man." His smile broadened. "Hope you don't think we're this wild and woolly all the time. Lynching at Sweetgrass; stage holdup at Gage's; livery-barn gunfight at Bozeman! Most of the time we're a peaceful, sober community."

"I'm sure you are, Mr. Alderson."

"What about last night? I'd like to have your version of it."

Perry Hamil chose his words carefully. To make it convincing he put on a rueful, self-deprecating grin. "I guess I must've got the buck ague, Mr. Alderson. My foreman tossed his gun to me, to hold while he worked on Hickey. Next I knew another man began shooting from the alley. I was scared stiff for a minute. But I had a gun in my hand and I popped away with it. Didn't hit anything, naturally. But Kendall did. He cut loose about the same time and dropped the guy. That's all there was to it."

Alderson nodded, wrote a few lines on a pad. "Walt Mason tells it the same way. And it's the only way that makes sense. I guess that Kendall boy just wants to be modest."

"Kendall? What does he say?"

"He seems to think his bullet missed and yours made the hit."

Hamil laughed. "Nonsense! I had the buck ague and couldn't've hit the side of a barn."

"The sheriff's office," Alderson agreed, "has already come to that conclusion. It stands to reason, Kendall being a cowboy with plenty of gun-savvy, while you . . ."

"While I'm a dub," Hamil finished for him. "Never touched a six-shooter in my life till Mason tossed that one to me last night. In the Navy we weren't armed with pistols. And the only firearm I ever used, back home in Virginia, was a shotgun for ducks."

The newsman was clearly convinced. He wrote rapidly on his pad and Hamil knew the story would be printed just that way. A girl named Diane, reading it at Roanoke, would have no reason to doubt the identity of a participant named as Barry Rodman.

"I might as well call you Barry," Alderson said. "Your uncle and I were close friends. If I remember rightly, he presented you with a year's subscription to the *Courier*. It still has a few months to run. I suppose you'll want us to mail it to the ranch now, instead of to Roanoke."

"No. Just keep sending it to Roanoke. Friends of mine there like to read it so they can keep track of me. I can take out another subscription for the ranch."

Davis & Davis, when Hamil called on them in the afternoon, raised no questions. They'd examined and filed his four papers of identification, and their unimaginative minds had rubber-stamped him as Barry Rodman of Virginia.

Yet Hamil left their office with two minor disappointments. Six months, they'd told him, was the minimum time required by law for advertising a notice of decease, so that any creditors could come forward with claims. For that long at least the bulk of the Rodman estate must remain in control of the executors.

"In the meantime you can't live on thin air, Barry my boy." Ridley Davis said it in a spirit meant to be tolerant and liberal. "So we'll advance you a hundred a month for pocket money. You'll hardly need any more, living out at the ranch most of the time."

Hamil had hoped for much more. It meant he'd be stuck here at least six months. Which wouldn't be so bad except for that girl Diane in the East. A girl waiting eagerly to be sent for!

Hamil's next stop was at the coroner's office, where he was needed as a witness at an inquest. Other witnesses were Walt Mason, Rolfe Kendall and Fridley's night man. All agreed that Roy Hickey had been shot by his partner in crime, Dutch Yeager; and that the motive had been to shut Hickey's mouth. "He admitted the steal," Walt Mason testified. "He said the contact man had a patch over an eye and looked part Indian. Before he could say more, Yeager drilled him."

The coroner was concerned only with death. So the matter of whose bullet had broken Yeager's arm didn't come up. Yeager himself was in jail on a murder charge.

After the inquest Mason handed Hamil a key. "It's to your uncle's room at the ranch house. Move in any time you like. Rolfe and I'll be ridin' back to the roundup."

"What about those hundred steers?"

The foreman shrugged. "They've been butchered by now. All we can do is look for a halfbreed with a patched eye."

"I'll keep my eyes open." Hamil promised.

For two days, keeping his room at the Laclede, Perry Hamil did just that. He kept his eyes open; but not for a one-eyed halfbreed.

His alertness was for danger signs of exposure. This first week of his masquerade was crucial. He couldn't be sure that someone who'd known Barry Rodman in Virginia, or in the Navy, wouldn't pop up to denounce him. Most of the two days he idled in the hotel lobby, watching the life of Bozeman as it passed him by.

On the third day came another letter from Diane — a letter alive with intimate confidences and romantic expectations . . . "The letter you mailed at Glendive has just reached me, dear . . . I can hardly wait to get your first one from Bozeman."

She'll wait a long time, Hamil thought grimly. For there'd be no letter from Bozeman. At this moment she thought it was on the way to her, and that after it would come a steady flow of others — love notes all traveling slowly by stage and river boat and train.

Hamil, burned today's letter. Already he'd destroyed the ones from the portmanteau. He must put her out of Barry Rodman's life with a smothering silence, much as he would use a wet blanket to snuff out a fire.

He stood at his room window staring down at Main Street. A horseman in a tall hat was riding by. By its jaded look the horse must have come a long way. The brim of the hat hid the man's face; but Hamil had a feeling he'd seen the horse before. And there was something familiar about that thigh-level holster with its black-butted gun.

He watched the man ride on to a hitchrack and dismount. It was at a building being used by county officers pending completion of a new courthouse. As the horseman dismounted Hamil saw his face. As he feared, it was Harry De Shon, once a trigger-quick marshal in Kansas!

Riding only by day on a tired mount, it had taken him till now to reach Bozeman. Would he stay here? Hamil hoped desperately that he wouldn't. At Huntley the man had almost recognized him. Hamil remembered the narrowed slant of his eyes, and his question, "Haven't I seen you before somewhere?"

He had, of course. Five years ago in a Kansas jail. Riding on toward Bozeman, had De Shon put a finger on that stray string of memory? Was he now telling tales to the sheriff?

For it was the sheriff's office which the man now entered. Hamil stared fearfully that way. There sat the law of Gallatin County! What was Harry De Shon, who'd been run out of Miles City as an undesirable citizen, doing in the sheriff's office at Bozeman?

A knock took Hamil to his door. A boy from the lobby handed in a paper. "You were asking for one this morning, Mr. Rodman; this one just came in."

It was a weekly published at Billings. Hamil looked through it and found a news item which had come by telegraph from Miles City.

The identification of Perry Hamil, one of the victims of the recent Sioux raid, has been confirmed. A horse abandoned by Hamil has been picked up near Miles City. The brand establishes it as a horse stolen by Hamil at El Paso, Texas. El Paso officers, in telegraphic communication with local authorities, describe Hamil as a long-wanted outlaw. No claim has been made for his body.

The news helped to relax Hamil. By now the body was buried and forgotten. All hazard from Texas was over and gone. The only hazards left were a girl in Virginia — and De Shon right here in Bozeman.

Hamil sucked nervously on a cigaret. Why the devil had De Shon stopped at the sheriff's office?

Again came a knock at the door. And again it was a boy from the lobby. The boy grinned. "Message from the sheriff's office, Mr. Rodman. He wants to see you right away."

A sense of being trapped came to Hamil. It could only mean one thing. De Shon had exposed him! ". . . That guy who came in on the Miles City stage the other day, claimin' to be a navy man from Virginia. He's a phony, Sheriff. Five years ago I kept him overnight in my jail, down at Dodge, Kansas . . ."

De Shon must have put it something like that. Obviously the local sheriff didn't believe it; otherwise he would have sent a deputy here to arrest Hamil.

A summons relayed through a bellboy meant that the sheriff was merely checking a report which, incredible as it was, still had to be cleared up as a matter of routine. When Hamil denied it, the sheriff would take his word over De Shon's.

But it wouldn't end there. If De Shon had talked once he'd talk again. The same remark at a bar would send a rumor around Bozeman. And even a slight whisper of doubt would put skids under Hamil. It would reach Davis & Davis, and they'd write Roanoke for an exact description of Barry Rodman.

Yet any delay in reporting to the sheriff would only quicken suspicions. With a sense of defeat Hamil went out. He'd deny everything. Then, during the few days it would take to check on him, he'd ride far and fast from Montana.

He walked into the sheriff's office braced to find De Shon there, ready to point a finger. But only Sheriff McKinzie himself was in the office. The officer sat at his desk, looking gray and tired.

The man smiled and held out a hand. "So you're John Rodman's nephew! Glad to know you, young man. I understand you just took on a new hand at the JR. Fella named Kendall."

"That's right. He left with Walt Mason to join the roundup."

"In that case he'll need his saddle." McKinzie nodded toward a stock saddle on the floor. "Better take it to the ranch, whenever you go out there. It's the one he lost at the stage holdup."

Relief swept over Hamil. Last seen, this saddle had been on the back of a stage horse with which the third of three horse thieves had escaped toward Crazy Mountain. "You caught him?"

"Nope, we didn't." The sheriff said it half sheepishly. "We chased him, but lost his tracks in Shields River. But when I got back to Bozeman this morning I found him sitting in this chair. Kendall's saddle lay on the floor and the stage horse was hitched outside."

"He gave himself up?"

"That's right."

"Where is he now?"

"In a cell waiting for a preliminary hearing before Judge Martin. It comes up in about an hour. Just to make the case airtight we need two witnesses. The stage driver's away on his run. Kendall's on roundup and Adam Cram's on a business trip to Helena. So I sent for you and Lucia Ripley. The two of you can identify him as the hold-up man."

Not a word about De Shon. Why had De Shon come in here? Hamil probed cautiously for an answer. "At Huntley we ran into a man named De Shon. Mr. Cram, Rolfe Kendall and I bunked with him there. Didn't I see him come in here?"

The sheriff stoked his pipe, nodding. "He's a peace officer by trade and he bit me for a deputy's billet. We're shorthanded; but I turned him down."

"Why?"

"Because he's one of those badge-wearing killers. His record's pretty well known even up here in Montana. The quicker he leaves town the better I'll like it."

In late afternoon a prisoner was brought in for a preliminary hearing before Judge Matthew Martin. A group of onlookers present included Alderson of the *Courier*. Perry Hamil, seated by the only other witness, Lucia Ripley, listened curiously. "State your name and age," the court prompted.

"I'm Kim Dallas," the prisoner answered. "I was nineteen last month."

Hamil saw a gentle sympathy on the face of the army girl beside him. Kim Dallas, haggard and bearded out on the stage road, had managed to get a shave and some sleep. Right now he looked like a frightened boy.

"You're charged," the court said, "with stealing horses from the H Bar ranch near Sweetgrass last Wednesday night, and with holding up a stage Friday morning, stealing a horse and saddle from said stage. How do you plead?"

"Innocent," the boy pleaded, "of what you claim. I did Wednesday night. And I can prove it. Ask White Calfee when he comes back with his mule train. All last Wednesday night I slept at his camp and had breakfast with him. In the morning the mule train went one way and I went the other. Mr. Calfee'll back me up on it."

"If he does," the judge told him, "the H Bar charge will be dropped. What about the stage job?"

"On the trail I met two men with some horses and rode along with them. We were camping on Sweetgrass Creek when a gang of men came at us. They had guns and ropes. I got away in the dark, afoot, and hid in the brush. There was a moon and I saw them lynch the two men I'd camped with. They were beating the bushes to do the same with me."

"So you held up a stage to steal a horse and saddle!"

"To borrow a horse and saddle. I brought 'em back, didn't I?"

"You borrowed them at the point of a gun." The judge turned toward the witnesses. "Miss Ripley, you were a passenger on the stage. Is this the man who held you up?"

The army girl got to her feet and to Hamil she looked flushed and angry. "He is. But that's not all I want to say, Judge Martin."

The judge gave her a tolerant smile. "Very well. If it pertains to this case, say anything you want."

"I saw two men hanging from a tree." Lucia faced the court, the flame in her cheeks matching the red of her hair. "I saw a mob at the stage station and I heard them say they'd lynch this one too, if they could catch him. We know now that up to that time he hadn't committed any crime. It would have been murder in cold blood and in this county. Yet I don't see those lynchers brought to trial here. I'm not being asked to identify *them*. This boy had a choice of being hanged for something he hadn't done, or of helping himself to a

97

horse and saddle by the only means possible. He brought the horse and saddle back. He gave himself up to the law. Assuming Mr. White Calfee confirms his innocence on last Wednesday night, I think this boy should be let off with a fine. And I'd like to pay that fine myself."

"I'm the judge," Martin said in a tone of mild rebuke. "You're only a witness. What about you, Mr. Rodman? Can you identify the prisoner?"

An inspired thought came to Hamil. He felt no sympathy for young Dallas. But here was a chance to build himself up with Lucia Ripley; and to get his name linked with hers in a news story.

"He did it, Judge," Hamil testified. "But suppose he hadn't? Where would he be now? He'd be hanging from a cottonwood on Sweetgrass Creek. He wouldn't say he camped all night with Calfee unless it was true. It's too easy checked on. So this boy not only saved his own neck, but he saved a lot of red faces." Hamil turned to Sheriff McKinzie. "Your face would be plenty red, wouldn't it, Sheriff, if an innocent boy got lynched right in your own county?"

McKinzie was a fair man. "I reckon it would, Mr. Rodman."

Hamil turned back to the judge. "I feel just like Miss Ripley does about this. Except if you let this kid off with a fine, I want to split it with her."

The judge looked uncomfortably from the prosecutor to the sheriff. He cleared his throat. "Do the people have any objections?"

The prosecutor spoke aside with the sheriff. Then both held a whispered conference with the judge. And as Perry Hamil sat down, Lucia took his hand and gave it a squeeze. He'd scored big with her.

And he sensed that the judge, prosecutor and sheriff were in a trap. They'd all three want to be re-elected in November. A too severe treatment of a boy who'd almost been lynched for something he hadn't done, with no arrests being made for lynchings actually committed, would win public sympathy for the boy, and exactly the opposite for the three county officers.

The judge rapped on his desk and made Kim Dallas stand up. "I'm going to waive the normal procedure and dispose of this case right here. Kim Dallas, I fine you two hundred dollars and direct that you be held in jail until White Calfee can be questioned about your alibi. If it stands up, you're to be set free at once. Court adjourned."

Lucia Ripley took a hundred dollars from her purse. Hamil produced the same amount from his own. Under the reportorial eye of Editor Alderson, they paid the fine on the spot. Then Lucia slipped her arm through Hamil's and they left the courtroom.

A buzz of whispers followed them. Hamil caught a phrase or two. "He carried her out of the river, down at Huntley."

It would all be in next week's *Courier*. He was getting every break, Hamil exulted. "Now that you're in town, what about supper tonight, Lucia?"

A hundred people on Main Street saw her look up at him and smile. "That's awfully nice of you, Barry. But I promised some friends to watch Guard Mount with them, out at the post. This is my rig."

Hamil handed her into the buggy she'd driven from Fort Ellis. "What about the box supper next week?" he persisted.

"One of the post officers is bringing me," Lucia said. "But you may bid on my box, if you like." She flapped her reins and drove off toward the post, only three miles east.

Yes, everything was breaking his way, Hamil thought as he went to a saloon for a drink. Going fifty-fifty on that fine was a neat trick. It would make them hero and heroine of a nice little human-interest story, all to be dished up in black and white for the reading of a girl in Virginia.

The saloon Hamil chose was the Delmonico. He stood at its elegant rosewood bar and as he sipped his drink bits of stray talk drifted to him. The bartender was dispensing information.

"So Chips hired the guy for a bouncer and spotter. He's got a rep, this guy has. Hell keep an eye out for sharpers and if anybody gets tough, he'll throw 'em out quick."

"I heard he tried to get on at the sheriff's office," a customer remarked, "but McKinzie turned him down. Is that him sittin' over there with Chips and Rhonda?"

Hamil looked that way, and saw three at a table. One was the platinum — blond hostess and another was Chips Charny himself. Before the rush of evening trade they were relaxing over drinks and getting acquainted with a new addition to the staff.

Harry De Shon! Hamil's first thought was: how are the mighty fallen! De Shon, once a famous town-taming marshal, now reduced to spotting cheaters and bouncing bums at a Bozeman bar!

Then the man's head turned and his eyes met Hamil's. A gleam of quizzical speculation made Hamil down his liquor so fast it almost choked him. Hurriedly he left the Delmonico, his confidence again dented. The only cure for De Shon was to stay out of his way.

CHAPTER
NINE

To stay out of the man's way, early the next morning Hamil hired a livery rig and had himself driven to the JR. The wrangler who drove him pointed out landmarks. "This here's Sourdough Crik. We foller it a piece south and then cut over a rise toward Middle Fork. That's Blackmore Mountain you see dead ahead. If you was atop of it you could see plumb into Yellowstone Park."

Hamil listened absently, his mind centered mainly on his own strategies of deception. Such as riding to his ranch in a livery rig, like a tenderfoot, instead of coming horseback like a Texan. Always he must be Barry Rodman, and never Perry Hamil.

The rig left Sourdough Creek and headed southwest. Pineclad slopes made walls in three directions. "Them snowy mountains ahead," the driver explained, "are Gallatin and Sphinx Peaks. The Virginia City gold diggin's lay beyond 'em."

They passed through a gate. "We're on Mike Lockhart's land now. Mike's got grass on both sides of yourn, Mr. Rodman. He was always pesterin' your uncle to sell out to him."

They passed through another gate and came into a lush valley. Across a pasture fence Hamil saw grazing horses with JR on them. Beyond was a line of cottonwoods and a cluster of painted roofs.

Presently they drove into a barnyard on the bank of a riffling river. There were sheds, corrals, bins, a windmill, a small white house and a big red stable. "Your uncle didn't believe in lettin' things run down." The liveryman waved a hand. "Hi, Pony! Hi, Charley! I brung out yer new boss." He braked to a stop at the house gate. "Here you are, Mr. Rodman. That there China-boy grinnin' in the doorway is Charley the cook; and this here's Pony Willard, your choreman."

Pony Willard was past sixty, knobby, grizzled, and walked with a limp. "Been expectin' you," he grinned. "Walt told me you'd be comin' out. I'll tote your bag in for you."

"Thanks; I'll handle it." Hamil took the portmanteau himself. Barry Rodman wouldn't have let an elderly cripple carry a bag for him; so neither must Perry Hamil.

After Charley served lunch, the liveryman unloaded Rolfe Kendall's saddle and drove back to town. Pony Willard returned to his chores and Hamil began exploring the house.

There were only four rooms. A large kitchen with a dining table at one end; a carpeted parlor; a small bedroom for guests; and a large locked room which had been John Rodman's.

A log bunkhouse across the yard made sleeping quarters for the help. Just now all hands except the cook and choreman were off on roundup.

Hamil used a key Walt Mason had given him and entered John Rodman's bedroom. It was a man's room, ruggedly furnished. The puncheon floor had only a pair of wolfskin. throw rugs on it. The chairs were backed with rawhide; the washstand had a china bowl and pitcher. There was a stand with a kerosene lamp. The bedspread had been made by patching beaver skins together. In an alcove stood a rolltop desk. This room had been both home and office for John Rodman. The only wall decoration was a calendar with a colored landscape on it, advertising A. Lamme & Co., Bozeman merchants.

The closet had suits and boots. Hamil tried on a corduroy coat and found it too tight. But a pair of almost new boots fitted perfectly.

What most took his eye was a gunbelt with a holstered forty-five. Hamil strapped it on and it gave him a sense of security. Ever since planting his own in a raided stagecoach, he'd felt awkward and helpless.

A desk drawer had several boxes of cartridges. Hamil filled the belt sockets and the cylinder of the gun. He wanted to keep wearing it. But how could he be Barry Rodman and carry a gun?

After a while of brooding Hamil summoned an answer. He went down to the corrals and found Pony Willard.

"Look, Pony." Hamil put on a wry grin. "Twice since I left Miles City I've been under gunfire without anything to shoot back with. And even if I'd had a gun, I couldn't've hit anything with it. I don't want to be caught like that again."

"Can't say's I blame yuh."

"I've found a gun of my uncle's and I want to do some practicing. Could you set up a target, somewhere?"

"I sure can. And it ain't a bad idea, neither. Feller can get in a tight corner, out here, if he don't have no gun on him. He's got to know how to use it, though."

"I found that out, the other night in a livery barn. Walt Mason gave me his gun to hold."

The choreman nodded sagely. "I heard about it. You shot wild and if it hadn't been fer that cowboy Kendall you'd've got your head blowed off. I'll go set up that target right now."

"Thanks. I'll be ready to start popping away, after a while."

Hamil spent an hour ransacking John Rodman's desk. What he most feared was a photograph of the Virginia nephew. A vast relief came when he failed to find anything but a small framed daguerreotype on a silver-coated plate. It showed a man and a woman, both youngish. Possibly the man was John Rodman's brother and the woman Barry Rodman's mother.

Since he couldn't identify the picture Hamil destroyed it. He must destroy every family record he couldn't understand.

In the desk he found two letters written by Barry Rodman to his uncle. The last one mentioned a girl named Diane Burgess. So her name was Burgess! The letter hinted at, but didn't announce, the nephew's engagement to her.

Most of the other papers had to do with business affairs. There was a record book which showed that John Rodman had paid thirty thousand dollars for the Rodman Block, and that rentals from it were bringing in nearly three hundred a month. A bank book showed sizable deposits but gave no present balance. And Hamil couldn't forget that Lockhart was offering sixty thousand for the ranch alone.

All of it mine, if I can keep them fooled another six months!

A phase of the fooling began an hour later, out in the barnyard. Perry Hamil stood facing a bull's-eye target which Pony had tacked on the outer wall of a shed. "It was left over from a turkey shoot we had last fall. Your uncle was a purty fair shot hisself."

But the nephew, apparently, wasn't. At a range of fifteen paces Hamil aimed to miss. The gun roared and a hole appeared in the shed planking, a good five feet wide of the bull's-eye.

Pony Willard observed critically. "Squeeze the trigger slow and easy next time."

Hamil pretended to try. But again and again he missed widely. The shots brought Charley from the kitchen, making a second reliable witness to some very bad shooting. Pony kept giving advice, but it was no use.

"You'd better stay out of bad company," the choreman said, "until you can do better 'n that."

"I'll keep practicin'," Hamil promised.

June was a week older when Walt Mason and Rolfe Kendall rode home from the roundup. It wasn't over yet — a spring roundup was rarely over before the first of July — but they'd left Mack Boyd there to rep for the JR.

As they cantered into the barnyard a target caught their attention. They rode to it for a closer look. The wall of a plank shed was riddled with bullet holes. The holes surrounded the target, except for a very few that had pierced the cardboard itself. The center circle hadn't a mark in it.

"Must've been Charley the cook," Walt remarked. "Nobody else could shoot that bad."

Pony Willard came limping up. "Nope, Walt, it was that new boss of ours, Barry Rodman. He's been at it all week, learnin' to shoot with his uncle's gun."

Mason and Kendall exchanged nods. To both it seemed reasonable. No one could blame the new owner for learning how to defend himself.

To Rolfe Kendall it cleared up something else. He'd been sure that it was Rodman's bullet, not his own, which had dropped Dutch Yeager. Now he was convinced it had been only a lucky hit, For here was clear proof that Barry Rodman had no skill with a gun.

"He's up at the house, Pony?"

"Nope. This afternoon he saddled up and lit out fer town. Nothin' wrong with his ridin', 'cept he don't cotton much to our stock saddles. He says Virginia's hoss country, all the same like Montana."

After a bath and a change, Walt and Rolfe loped off toward Bozeman. Something special was on there tonight. Nightfall caught them as they neared town.

Walt spurred on impatiently; and Rolfe, smiling in the dark, knew why.

They found Main Street lined with rigs and saddle mounts. From lighted windows on the second floor of the Rodman Block came gay music and laughter. The season's most important party was on at Chestnut Hall. There'd be an auction supper, and dancing till dawn. For weeks the *Courier* had been beating the drums for it.

Guns weren't allowed on the dance floor, so the two JR men left theirs at Fridley's barn. Presently they were pushing their way through the crowd at Chestnut Hall.

The entire county was on hand; ranch folk, town folk, army folk. Fort Ellis had always taken a prominent part in the social life of Bozeman. Fifty couples were on the floor with as many more lining the walls. Rolfe glimpsed Lucia Ripley as she whirled by in the arms of a second lieutenant in formal uniform.

Her smile as she passed was not for Rolfe but for Walt Mason. The JR foreman took an eager step forward. "Next one, Lucia?" She didn't hear him and was lost in the crowd.

Then the music stopped and the bidding began. Women were herded to one end of the hall, men to the other. The Honorable Martin Maginnis himself, the territory's delegate to Congress, acted as auctioneer.

Rolfe Kendall stayed out of it. Lucia was the only girl he knew and he didn't want to bid against Walt. Walt had a full month's pay in his pocket and a determined set to his jaw.

Most of the supper baskets went for less than six dollars. The general run of ranch boys couldn't afford more than that. The basket of a pretty brunette from Spring Hill brought nine dollars; one prepared by a buxom Bridger Creek blonde brought ten. At each successful bid the Bozeman Silver Cornet Band gave a fanfare of trumpets.

As each man bid for a basket, he advanced to offer his arm to the lady who'd brought it. The couple then marched from the hall, crossing Main Street to a feast at the Laclede Hotel.

The crowd in the hall grew smaller. Lucia's basket hadn't been offered yet. Three determined young men had eyes on it. Rolfe, idling near the exit, heard whispers.

"That second louee'll get her, all right. He drove her in, didn't he? And he makes more money than Walt does."

"Yeh, but what about that guy from Virginia? He packed her outa the river down at Huntley; and he's been shinin' up to her ever since."

Another fanfare and Auctioneer Maginnis clapped for silence. "Gentlemen, we're saving the best till the last." He held up a beribboned basket, sniffed at it. "Smells like fried chicken and wild currant pie. Purtiest girl at the fort goes with it. Which one of you boys feels lucky? And don't forget, it's all for the hospital fund."

"Five dollars," Walt Mason offered.

"Ten." The second lieutenant had a confident smile.

"Twenty." The army man's jaw dropped when a rank outsider doubled his bid.

"Twenty-one." Mason raised it cautiously. Then the Fort Ellis man echoed him with a raise to twenty-five.

"Thirty." The new owner of the JR ranch kept boosting it.

At forty dollars Walt Mason dropped out. It was all he had in pocket and bids must be paid promptly in cash.

The lieutenant kept at it. Lucia was his date and he'd lose face if he let a rival take her to supper.

"Fifty."

"Fifty-two."

"Sixty."

"Sixty-one."

"Seventy." The man they knew as Barry Rodman kept raising recklessly.

With a wry smile the lieutenant dropped out. The man who'd outbid him picked up Lucia's basket, gave Lucia his arm and marched her in triumph from the hall. The biggest fanfare of the night blared from the band. Rolfe saw Alderson of the *Courier* making notes. To promote the hospital fund, the more generous bids would be published as a matter of news.

"Cheer up, Walt," Rolfe said. "Come along and I'll buy you a drink."

Halfway down the stairs they met a deputy coming up. "Hello, Walt. Sheriff McKinzie wants to see you a minute. You too, Kendall."

"What's up?"

"Search me. It's something you oughta know, the sheriff says."

They found McKinzie in his office facing a prisoner he'd just released from a cell. Rolfe recognized the boy who'd held up the stage near Gage's Ranch.

"This is Kim Dallas," McKinzie explained. "The judge told me to keep him locked up till White Calfee backed up an alibi. Calfee's mule train's at Miles City now and we just got in touch with him by wire. He says the boy told us the truth. So I'm setting him free."

Mason looked the boy over. The story of a courtroom scene, with two sympathetic witnesses paying a fine, had reached the roundup camp. "Where do *we* come in?" the foreman asked curiously.

"Tell them what you just told me, Kim," McKinzie directed.

"I've been locked up for ten days," Kim Dallas told them, "and in the next cell was a man named Yeager. He's waiting trial for murder. First day I was there he got chummy and talked to me through the bars. He knew I'd held up a stage and was charged with stealing horses; so he figured he and I were birds of a feather."

"He naturally would," Rolfe agreed. "So he got chummy. What did he say?"

"He said he wanted me to help him break out, when the right time came. He claimed he has a backer right here in Bozeman who'll smuggle him in a gun soon as his arm heals enough to use it. With that gun and my help, he could crack down on the jailer when he came with grub, grab the keys and crash out. He said he'd take me to a hideaway where they'd never find us."

"What did you say?"

"I asked who this backer was who's going to smuggle him in a gun. He said he's one of the top men around here, with plenty of money and influence."

"What else?"

"That's all. Next day he heard I'd gotten off with a fine and would soon be turned loose. So he clammed up. I was afraid to tell the jailer, because Yeager was in the next cell and would hear me. But the minute they let me out I told the sheriff."

"I'm cutting you in on it, Walt," McKinzie said, "because the JR lost a hundred steers to Yeager and whoever's backing him. Got any ideas?"

"I sure have," Walt answered promptly. "I just came from the roundup and some of the tallies make this thing look bigger than we thought. Charley Anceney had a small bunch of steers up Spanish Creek, or thought he had, and they're missing too. MacAndow Brothers report two hundred three-year-old beeves missing from a pocket just below Windy Pass. Dave Fratt can't find some he-stuff he thought he had up Cottonwood Creek. All these losses have two points in common."

McKinzie cocked an eye. "Which are?"

"In each case the loss was all he-stuff. Mature beef. And in each case the thieves must've had inside information. Someone on the payroll of each ranch who tipped 'em about a bunch of steers pushed off on some out-of-the-way pocket of grass. We don't treat cow-and-calf stuff like that between March and June; it has to be kept on lower ground and watched closer. But you can shove mature steers into some mountain park,

112

if it's got untouched grass left over from last year, and not worry too much about April and May snowstorms."

"It adds up to an organized gang," McKinzie brooded. "A gang that's got a beef market somewhere. And a backer right here in Bozeman."

"This backer," Kim Dallas repeated, "is some top citizen with money and influence."

McKinzie and Mason fell into brown studies. Rolfe Kendall knew that each was checking over in his mind the county's wealthiest and most influential men.

"Couldn't be Nelson Story or Mike Lockhart," Walt muttered. "They've both got money and influence; but they're both on the up and up. Same goes for Dilworth and Jeffers."

McKinzie pursed his lips. "We can rule out Anceney, Fratt and the MacAndows, Walt, because they lost some stuff same as the JR. What about merchants here in town?"

Mason tapped off on his fingers the more important storekeepers. "Tracy, Willson, Rich,. Lamme — they're all on the level. I can't figure Adam Cram for a crook, either."

Rolfe had a thought. "What about saloon owners? To a toughie like Yeager, anyone who runs a fancy bar would rate high."

"You mean Chips Charny?"

"I don't know him. Does he fit the bill?"

"He's got money," McKinzie admitted. "Made it tradin' red-eye and rifles to the Sioux. But he hasn't got any influence — except with dance girls and dice sharks."

"Just the kind of people," Rolfe suggested, "that he'd use if he wanted to smuggle a gun to Yeager."

The sheriff smiled grimly. "He'll have a helluva time getting one in now, after this warning from Kim Dallas."

In a little while Mason, Kendall and Dallas left the office. On the front walk Mason asked, "Got any plans, Kim?"

The boy nodded. "I got some folks who want to come west next spring in a covered wagon. They'll want to file on land. So in the morning I'll start looking for a good bottomland half section."

"You got a horse?"

"Yeh. Those lynchers cut me off from it that night on Sweetgrass Creek; but Sheriff McKinzie picked it up later and brought it to town."

"Okay." Walt gave him a pat on the shoulder. "Make the JR your headquarters, if you like, while you're spotting some land for your people to file on next season. Just tell Pony Willard I sent you and he'll show you a bunk."

Rolfe shot a quick, approving look at his foreman. Walt had the right stuff in him, all right. That army girl could go a lot farther and do worse.

"Thanks a lot," Kim said. "Right now I've got to look up Miss Ripley and Barry Rodman. Sheriff said they're at the Laclede eating supper."

"That's right. What do you want to see them about?"

"Just want to tell 'em," Kim said, "that I'll pay back every cent of those fines. A little each month, soon as I can earn it."

114

He started diagonally across the street, angling toward the Laclede Hotel. Walt and Rolfe stood on the walk, looking shrewdly after him. "That kid'll turn out all right," Walt predicted, "if I'm any judge of —"

He got no further. A rifle shot cracked from the night. Rolfe saw a flash of flame and it seemed to come from a rooftop half a block west. At the same moment Kim Dallas crumpled in the Main Street dust.

CHAPTER
TEN

Walt ran toward Kim. Rolfe took the opposite direction, west up the sidewalk toward where he'd seen the flash of a sniper's rifle. After a few steps he stopped, remembering he was unarmed.

Sheriff McKinzie burst from his office with a gun in hand. "Didn't I hear a shot?"

Rolfe pointed. "It came from that roof. Where can I get a gun?"

"Help yourself." The sheriff jerked a thumb toward the open door of his office. Then he ran toward the next corner west.

Rolfe dashed into the sheriff's office. On a wall of it were four racked rifles; posse guns to be used in an emergency. He took one, pumped a shell into its chamber and went out to race after McKinzie.

The next corner west was the crossing of Black Street and Main. A saloon, a furniture store and the Northern Pacific Hotel occupied three corners. On the fourth, and operated in connection with the hotel, was the Northern Pacific livery stable. The stable had a flat roof and a false parapet front. Rolfe was sure the shot had been fired from behind that parapet.

116

McKinzie was at the barn's entrance firing questions at the night man. The night man had heard the shot. It had seemed to come from overhead. There was no ladder to the room. He didn't know how a man could get up there. McKinzie said: "I brought a prisoner's horse back from Sweetgrass Creek last week. Left it in a stall here till the man could be turned loose. Did anybody ask about it?"

"Not since I came on duty, Sheriff."

Rolfe didn't linger to hear more. He ran up Black Street to a corral behind the barn. A wagon loaded with baled hay was parked along the barn's rear wall. A few of the bales had been unloaded to feed horses inside. The missing bales had left convenient steps by which a man could climb to the load's top, and from there to the barn roof.

No use looking for him there now. The sniper would have come down at once. Which way would he go?

He might circle to Main Street and lose himself in a crowded barroom; or slip away in darkness to some backstreet cabin; or run to his horse, riding far and fast out of Bozeman.

McKinzie, looking gaunt and tired, loomed in the dimness beside Rolfe. "It figures," he muttered grimly. "That backer Dutch Yeager bragged about. He was afraid Dutch mentioned his name and so he had the boy picked off the minute he got out of jail."

Rolfe gave a shrewd nod. "They found out you'd stabled Kim's horse here. It was a fair bet that Kim would come right here to get it when he was turned loose. So a killer waited on the roof to pick him off."

117

The sheriff sighed. "That sniper's a long way from here by now. No chance to track him before morning." And not even then, Rolfe thought. Because a hundred horsemen, tonight, were making tracks to and from Bozeman. "Let's take a look on the roof, Sheriff."

Using the stepped hay bales for stairs they climbed to the stable's roof. At the front, behind the false parapet, McKinzie picked up an empty shell. It was from a 44 — 40 rifle. Then Rolfe struck a match for a closer look. A dozen cigaret butts were strewn about. The smokes had all been made with brown paper.

"What callers has Yeager had, Sheriff?"

"Only his lawyer; and the doctor who treated his arm."

For a moment it puzzled Rolfe. Assuming the lawyer and doctor were law-abiding people, how had Yeager managed to send word to his backer that Kim Dallas knew too much?

The point drew a simple explanation from McKinzie. "Yeager's cell has a small, high, barred window for ventilation. It gives to an alley. A man could slip up in the dark; by standing on a box he could talk with Yeager through the bars; or even slip him a gun."

"I see. The gun hasn't been slipped in yet because Yeager has a busted arm. They're waitin' till it heals."

"We'll move Yeager to an inside cell," McKinzie promised, "and search anyone who comes to see him."

They climbed down from the roof. McKinzie hurried off to question anyone on either Main or Black Street who might have glimpsed the rifleman before or after the shot.

118

Rolfe crossed Black and entered an east-and-west alley. Halfway along it he came to the back of the jail. There was a row of small barred windows all higher than a man's head. A pile of packing boxes lay behind a shop next door. Rolfe carried one of them to a cell window and stood on it. The cell was empty. It might be the one from which Kim Dallas had just been released.

Moving his box to the next vent Rolfe again peered through bars. This time he saw Yeager, with his arm in a sling, sitting on a cot. An emissary from the "rich and influential" backer could have talked with Yeager through this vent. Yeager would warn his caller about Dallas; he'd admit he'd talked too much, judging his jail neighbor for a horse thief and road agent. Had he mentioned the backer by name? Maybe Yeager wasn't sure whether he had or not. In any case the safe thing would be to shut Kim's mouth.

Rolfe returned the packing box. Then he searched the ground below Yeager's window. Two faded cigaret butts were there, each made from brown paper.

So Yeager's dark-of-the-moon visitor was also the rooftop rifleman! A chain-smoker of brown-paper cigarets, armed with a 44-40 saddle gun. Was he loping away to some hideout? Or still in town?

Rolfe could think of one good reason why the man would still be in town. He couldn't have had a personal grudge against Kim Dallas. Therefore he was a hired killer. Hired killers usually weren't paid in advance. At least not in full. They had to earn the fee before being paid off. If that was the case tonight, the killer might want to collect before leaving town.

He'd collect from a man with money and influence. Mason and McKinzie had tossed a few names about, and the only one they hadn't eliminated was Chips Charny. Which left a bare chance that the sniper would call on Charny, this very night, to collect!

It was the only fertile idea Rolfe could summon. He continued through the alley and came out of it at Fridley's barn. There he retrieved his gunbelt and gun.

Then he went to McKinzie's office and put the rifle back on its rack. He'd look too much like a posseman if he went into Charny's place with a rifle.

Only a jailer was in McKinzie's office. "What about the boy?" Rolfe asked.

"He's still breathin'," the jailer said. "The slug went clean through him but Doc Monroe says he's got a chance."

"Where did they take him?"

"To that room up over Langhorne's drugstore they use for a hospital sometimes. Monroe's doin' everything he can. Barry Rodman and that army girl came over from the hotel. Nobody feels like frolicin' any more. It like to broke up the party."

As Rolfe moved on toward the Delmonico he saw a crowd in front of a drugstore. A sober crowd of town folk, ranch folk, army folk. A red-haired girl in a party dress moved among them passing a hat. It was the flat black hat of Barry Rodman. They were taking up a collection to pay for whatever medical attention was needed by Kim Dallas. "I'm sure you want to

120

contribute, Mr. Bowers," Lucia said. The man she addressed dropped a five-dollar bill into the hat.

Rolfe went into the Delmonico and found it full to the last inch of bar space. He had to reach over a man's shoulder to buy a beer. Rolfe carried it across the room and leaned against a wall. Every chair and table was occupied and every game board had a circle of players.

A medley of talk came to Rolfe and some of it was about the rooftop shot. "It was one of those Sweetgrass lynchers," a man guessed. "He still figures this kid's a horse thief and he's sore because they let him off with a fine."

"That ain't the way I heard it, Chuck. They claim some pard of Dutch Yeager done it. They say Dutch got too confidential with this kid. Three cards, Chuck, and it's your bet."

Chips Charny, short, wide and flashily garbed, moved about among his customers. A waxen smile never left his broad, tight-skinned face. His vest had brown and green checks with a heavy watch chain spanning it. He stopped in front of Rolfe Kendall. "You look lonesome, my friend. Shall I send you a hostess?"

"Never mind."

The saloonman moved on and presently Rolfe saw him disappear into a manager's office. Others of the staff kept in sight — dealers, a piano player, a blond hostess in a formal gown and three short-skirted house girls. Then Rolfe saw Harry De Shon; remembered him from the night when a stage had been stranded at Huntley; and from a news story describing him as an ex-town tamer from Kansas who lately had bested a man in a Miles City gunfight.

He looked the part, Rolfe thought, with that gun sagging low on his leg. The man's sharp black eyes kept sweeping from game to game. When the barkeeper slid him a drink De Shon didn't pay for it. So he was a house man, Rolfe concluded.

The man's eyes met Kendall's and narrowed briefly, as though he remembered Rolfe's face from Huntley.

One of the house girls came up and coaxed for a drink. "Not tonight," Rolfe said. She went poutingly away.

A man came in and passed Rolfe on his way to the bar. Rolfe wouldn't have noticed him except for the brown-paper cigaret hanging from his lip. The man had an unhealthy look and a flat chest. Except for dark circles under his eyes the skin of his face had a fish-belly pallor. He wore spurless boots and a loose sack coat. If he had a gun it was under the coat.

Brown-paper cigarets were common enough. But this man began rolling another before the one on his lip was finished. A chain smoker. Did he have a horse at the hitchrack? A saddle with a 44-40 in the scabbard?

Rolfe watched the man narrowly as he squeezed to a place at the bar and ordered whisky. Before picking it up he lighted the second cigaret. He sipped the drink stingily and by the time he finished it he was building still another brown-paper smoke. Could he be the rooftop sniper, here to collect a fee?

Glancing toward the rear Rolfe saw that Chips Charny had come out of his office. He was spelling one

122

of the house men. While the regular dice-table man took a rest, the owner himself took over, tossing dice or fading bets for the house.

The man with the sallow skin sauntered back that way. Rolfe tagged along himself, alert for any contact with Chips Charny. Five players were at the table, taking turns with the dice. When one of them quit, the man with the sallow skin took his place.

Rolfe watched closely for some sign of recognition between him and Charny. There wasn't any. Charny treated him impersonally. Apparently the new player was a stranger here.

Rolfe, missing nothing, saw him pick up the dice and drop ten dollars on the green. He was faded and tossed a four and a three. He let the stakes lie and again the house covered his bet. Again the man with a fish-belly pallor made a pass and again he let the winnings lie.

Again Chips Charny, as house man, faded the bet.

The customer made eight straight passes, letting the pot double every time. An unheard of run of luck! By the time it was over half the room was crowding around the dice board. Rolfe had to stand on tiptoe to see the play. A buzz of talk ran along the bar. The blond hostess appeared near Rolfe with De Shon at her elbow. "Chips is having a bad night, Harry," the woman murmured. "Pasty-face is nicking his roll."

De Shon smiled thinly. "It's a crapshooter's dream, Rhonda. But I can't collar the guy. Chips himself furnished the dice."

After the eighth straight pass a heap of currency lay on the table. Rolfe made a quick computation. A ten-spot doubled seven times would build up to twelve hundred and eighty dollars!

He saw the man scoop it up, stuff it into his pockets and walk out.

If it was blood money, it was the slickest pay-off ever made. No one would ever be able to prove that Charny had lost on purpose, by pre-arrangement, with the simple expedient of slipping his customer loaded dice. Everyone in the Delmonico, including the hostess and spotter, seemed convinced that the customer had won by a sheer run of luck.

Everyone but Rolfe Kendall. And even Rolfe would have been convinced except for the brown-paper cigarets.

He followed the man out and saw him stop on the walk to build another one. Off he went puffing it, west along Main. The man crossed Black Street, passed a frame hotel, the big Lamme store and the Tivoli beer hall.

He crossed Tracy Street, beyond which there were no more board walks or lighted shops. Rolfe didn't dare follow too closely. Now, in a cloudy darkness, he could neither see nor hear the man ahead. Sidewalks of hard-packed earth gave up no thumps from the man's boots.

But two blocks beyond Tracy a flicker of light led Rolfe on. The sallow man was holding a match to another cigaret. A block further on the man turned south on a side street. Rolfe glimpsed him in the dim light of a red lantern warning against an excavation just dug for the basement of the new courthouse.

So Rolfe also turned south on a street which had only an occasional frame residence or log cabin. In the pitch dark he could see nothing, and for two blocks south of Main he heard nothing. Then he caught a click, like the unlatching of a gate.

Rolfe moved on past a weed-grown lot. Beyond it he heard a door open and close. Ten steps more and he came to a yard fence. He groped along it to a picket gate. Then a lamp glow appeared at a window. Rolfe saw the shape of a small log cabin. The dicer's whitish face showed briefly at the window. Then the man jerked a shade down and Rolfe saw him no more.

Was he alone in there? Rolfe stood at the gate, unsure of his next move. The cabin's nearest neighbor was a two-story frame residence half a block east. This far out the town was only sparsely built. There was as yet no solid reason to accuse the man in there. Plenty of men smoked brown-paper cigarets; and the winnings could have been pure luck.

Rolfe stepped over the gate and moved quietly to the porch. There he listened for a sound of talk inside. When none came he concluded that the man was alone. The cabin was small; probably it only had one or two rooms.

Twin thumps reached Rolfe and they sounded like a man taking off his boots. A minute later the lamp glow disappeared from a window shade. Then silence. The man inside had clearly gone to bed.

Rolfe circled to the back and found a shed. A poultry smell came from it but no life was in the shed now. The yard was high with weeds and in general the place had

125

an abandoned look. The man inside might be a drifter who'd simply moved into a cabin left vacant by some nonresident owner.

A look at it in daylight should give better answers. The place could be watched to see who called here; or it could be searched if the man took a walk downtown. Breaking in on him now wasn't to be thought of. With all that money in his pockets the man would have locked his doors. At the first sound of a prowler he'd begin shooting.

Rolfe marked the corner — two blocks south of the new courthouse site. It was almost midnight when he withdrew quietly to the Northern Pacific Hotel. He signed the book and took a single room. "Call me at daybreak," he said to the clerk.

At gray dawn he was up and out. An open-all-night Chinese restaurant gave him breakfast. Walt Mason and Barry Rodman, he supposed, had taken rooms at the Laclede. For a moment Rolfe considered waking them up. Then he remembered the party at Chestnut Hall; and a life-or-death crisis for Kim Dallas. One or the other would have kept his friends up nearly all night.

Let them sleep. He'd look them up the minute he found out something more about that cabin. Rolfe checked the loads in his hip gun and hurried that way. This time he approached it along a street paralleling Main and two blocks south. He stopped a block short of it behind the screen of a board fence. An irrigation ditch from. Sourdough Creek ran along here and its overflow muddied a cow lot beyond the fence. A cow there had a swollen bag and was mooing for her calf.

Soon someone would come to milk the cow and Rolfe could ask him who lived in that log cabin just to the west.

The cow lot itself belonged to a tall frame residence with generous verandas — probably the town house of some important cattleman. Others like it were along this street, east of here. But west there were only a few scattered log cabins.

The one Rolfe watched had a pipe chimney. He'd see smoke there if the man made his breakfast. Half an hour passed and the chimney remained smokeless. Then the cabin's door opened and the man with the shallow face came out. He was dressed exactly as he had been last night, with no gun in sight.

He passed through the gate and turned toward Main. With twelve hundred and eighty dollars in his pockets, why should he cook his own breakfast?

When he was out of sight Rolfe advanced to the cabin and tried its door. It was locked, and so was a door at the back. Each side of the cabin had a window and Rolfe tried them all. All were locked. But one of the shades wasn't all the way down and peering through it Rolfe saw a rifle. It looked like a 44-40 Winchester.

The rifle stood in a corner of a room that had a table and an unmade cot. The floor was bare. A saucer by the cot was full of brown cigaret butts. A closet door stood half open. Another inside door was closed and probably gave to the cabin's kitchen. In this front room Rolfe could see only a shabby satchel, a canvas saddle roll and clothing hanging from pegs.

The 44-40 rifle doubled his suspicions. A search of the cabin might produce other clews to the man's character and connections. If he was last night's hired killer he must be nailed at once. Rolfe was in no mood to waste time. The man would be at a Main Street restaurant for at least half an hour.

So Rolfe Kendall drew his gun and tapped out a segment of glass. It made a hole through which he reached to unlock the window. After pushing up the sash he climbed into the room.

First he looked at the rifle. It was a 44-40 all right. A whiff at its breach told him it had been recently fired.

Next he went through the satchel. It had shirts and socks, a deck of cards and some dice. There was nothing to show that the man was anything but a tramp gambler. It was the same when Rolfe spread out the canvas saddle roll.

He looked into the closet. It had a slicker, a dirty sweater and an extra pair of boots. A shoe box on the closet's shelf caught Rolfe's eye and he took it down for a look.

What he found left him breathless and sent a sting of excitement through him. Here was proof, solid and convincing! Wait till he showed this to Walt Mason!

The box had three items. A black leather eye patch with an elastic band to hold it in place; a bottle of dark brown make-up stain; and a wig with neck-length locks of straight black hair.

Exactly what a man would need to make himself look like a half Indian with a patched eye. It meant that Sallow Face was the man who'd passed money to

Dutch Yeager and Roy Hickey, in March, for which they'd driven a hundred steers up the wrong creek. To Rolfe it tied everything in a knot. Sallow Face had talked through cell bars to Yeager; and later Yeager's backer had hired him to shoot down Kim Dallas.

More than likely Chips Charny was backing the whole play and had paid the killer by letting him make eight straight passes. But that part of it, Rolfe admitted, would need a bit more proof. He'd better look around for something to put a rivet in it; something that would stand up in court. As things stood now, a bald denial from Charny would be all the defense needed.

What about that hideaway Yeager had mentioned to Kim Dallas? Maybe this cabin had some clew to it; maybe a map or note of instructions; or mention of some out-of-the-way ranch or mine.

The kitchen might have something. Rolfe tried the door leading to the back room, found it locked. He turned to wall pegs to go through pockets of coats hanging there. Sallow Face might come back before he finished, but that didn't worry Rolfe now. He rather hoped the man would. For now he had proof that the man was at least a beef thief. He could put a gun on him and march him to McKinzie.

Rolfe went through a coat and a pair of pants. The pockets had nothing of importance. He took a second pair of pants from a peg, then noticed that it had longer legs than the other pair. Two coats had a different shoulder spread. They couldn't be worn by the same man.

All along Rolfe had been assuming that Sallow Face was the cabin's only occupant. Suddenly he realized that *two* men lived here. A big man and a little man. What about the other room? It too could have a cot and a man could be sleeping there right now.

Rolfe's back was to the door. As he turned he saw a gun leveled at him. The door leading to the other room was open. The man who stood in it was tall and broad and hairy. His cocked gun had a bead on Rolfe's chest. "Put 'em up slow and easy," the man said. He was in undershirt and sock feet. "It's my drop." He advanced soundlessly toward Rolfe. "Want to argue about it?"

"I know when I'm covered." Rolfe forced a grin and raised his hands ear-high. He wondered if anyone had gone out to milk that cow, in the lot just west of here; and if a gunshot would bring him running.

The hairy man's eyes had a wise gleam. "You're prowlin' for that roll Jody won last night, huh? I was there myself and I seen you lookin' on. Well, it's not here. Jody took it downtown with him."

So the big man had been in Charny's bar last night and had come home later than Jody. For that reason he'd slept later this morning. Rolfe decided that his safest choice was to let himself be mistaken for a thief on the prowl after Jody's winnings. On that count they might not kill him. If they knew his real errand they would.

"Okay; it looked like an easy pickup but I flubbed it. You got me cold, mister." They might take him to the sheriff, Rolfe thought hopefully, turning him in for a sneak thief.

130

It could have worked out just that way if the big man hadn't noticed an open shoe box. Beside it lay an eye patch, a long-haired wig and a bottle of brown stain. One look at it was enough. The man's gun barrel crashed hard on Rolfe Kendall's head and dropped him senseless to the floor.

CHAPTER
ELEVEN

A splitting headache was Rolfe's first sense of reality when he came to in the back room. Rawhide laces knotting his wrists and ankles made him helpless. He lay on a cot and an alarm clock near it said nine-thirty. The window shade was bright with daylight so it was still morning. He'd been out about three hours.

In a little while he heard movement in the front room. Then voices. The first voice, truculently impatient, was strange to Rolfe. "What the hell are we waiting for, Hunker?"

"Keep your shirt on, Jody. Clint says we dassent move him till dark."

Hunker would be the big man with the hairy chest. Jody was Sallow Face back from breakfast. Apparently Hunker had gone to get orders from somebody named Clint. Clint could be the backer with money and influence mentioned by Yeager.

To Rolfe, Clint's decision made sense. Moving him from this cabin, dead or alive, would be too big a risk in daylight. But after dark he could be hauled away in a wagon.

Which gave him a respite of ten or more hours. Walt Mason and Barry Rodman must have missed him by now. McKinzie would tell them where he'd last seen Rolfe — climbing down from a roof by way of a hay load.

What then? Mason might inquire at the bars and learn that Rolfe had stopped in briefly at the Delmonico. Nothing could have gone wrong there, the foreman would reason, because an hour later his missing hand had taken a room at a hotel where he'd slept all night.

They'd find that Rolfe's horse was still at Fridley's barn. But he'd called there for his gun. So Rolfe was still in town, armed and on foot.

The clews would end right there — unless someone had seen the missing cowboy just after dawn, walking toward the southwest edge of town.

The door opened and Hunker looked in. After a derisive stare the man closed the door and Rolfe heard him report: "He's come alive, Jody. And for the time being that's the way Clint wants it."

"Why?"

"Don't ask me. Ask Clint. You can bet he's got something up his sleeve. He's a smarty, Clint is; and he needs this guy for a chip."

For a long time Rolfe pondered over it. Why would Clint want him alive? He'd heard no mention of Charny. There was still no proof that Charny had paid off a killer by letting him win at dice. Rolfe tried desperately to fit the pieces; but his head was throbbing and his thoughts wouldn't mesh.

Through a torturing day he watched the clock. Bits of talk came to him but they added nothing to what had been said. At sundown Hunker came in with a glass of milk. He raised his prisoner to a sitting position and let him drink it. "Whose idea is it?" Rolfe asked. "Babyin' me like this."

"Not mine," Hunker said. "If it was left to me you'd be dumped in the Gallatin River."

A little later Rolfe heard one of his jailers leave by the front door. The window shade slowly blackened as daylight faded. At a few minutes after nine o'clock Rolfe heard wheels grinding on gravel.

Both Hunker and Jody came in, Hunker with a tolerant grin, Jody gunslung and ugly. The bigger man tied a blindfold over Rolfe's eyes. "We got a good night for it, Jody. No moon. Pick him up and let's ramble."

Jody took Rolfe by his bound feet and Hunker took a grip at the shoulders. Rolfe felt himself being carried out. His head bumped hard as they tossed him into the bed of a wagon. "Cover him with that tarp, Jody."

When the vehicle began moving, Rolfe judged by its springiness that it was either a buckboard or a spring wagon. By hoof sounds he could tell it was a two-horse team but there was no way of knowing the direction. No street sounds reached him. They'd keep to some deserted back street till they cleared the town. The tarp was tucked neatly around Rolfe, like a shroud, so even without the blindfold he would have been unable to see anything.

This street was deep-rutted, bumpy, but the same was true of all streets in Bozeman. Even the main stage roads were like this. For a little way the team moved at a trot, then settled to a plodding walk. "Keep an eye on

134

him, Jody; if he tries to wiggle out, bash him down. Giddap."

"He ain't stirrin' none," Jody said. "Looks like he's out cold."

It meant Hunker was driving. Where? To that unfindable hideaway mentioned by Yeager to Kim Dallas? Rolfe kept alert for more talk. They'd cheated his eyes but he still had ears.

The most likely direction would be south. To the north lay farming country and the settlements of Spring Hill, Reece Creek and East Gallatin. To the south were high, timbered mountains. Southward lay a trackless wilderness around and beyond Hyalite Park, where in March the man Jody, made up as a patched-eye halfbreed, had arranged the disappearance of a hundred JR steers.

Yet Rolfe had no more than reached that conclusion when a sound suddenly fixed his exact position. A sound close by and directly to the right of this trail. The clear notes of a bugle blowing Call to Quarters!

So they were passing the Fort Ellis stockade! Which meant they were just three miles due east of town, on the stage road to Bozeman Pass! The bugle call even fixed the exact minute. Taps was at ten o'clock on most army posts, with Call to Quarters usually blown fifteen minutes earlier.

Hunker whipped his team to a trot. "Reckon he heard that, Jody?"

"He still ain't stirrin' none," Jody reported. "Like I said, that bump on the bean must've knocked him out."

"Save us a heap of trouble," Hunker observed cheerfully, "if he'd croak. I don't envy Tuck none, wetnursin' him up there." He slowed his team as they approached some obstacle; and presently a splash of water told Rolfe they were fording a stream. It had to be the East Gallatin, since they were on the stage road to Bozeman Pass.

Rolfe tried hard to remember landmarks. He'd traveled this trail only once before, on a stage with Lucia Ripley, Adam Cram and Barry Rodman, a little more than a week ago. Sixteen years ago; according to Lucia, John Bozeman himself had come this way on his path-finding race with Jim Bridger.

Their last change stop before reaching Bozeman, Rolfe remembered, was Ten Mile, a station a little way this side of the pass.

The team kept plodding on, upgrade and always at a walk. Rolfe had no way to measure time or space. He remembered the stage road had left the main canyon in order to find an easier grade through a narrow, dry ravine.

About two hours dragged by. Then Rolfe heard roadside sounds; a stamping and champing of horses a few paces to the left. They could be saddle horses tied in front of Ten Mile station; some ranch hands could be at the bar there. Hunker didn't stop. Then another splashing of hooves again indicated a stream crossing. Jackson Creek, Rolfe remembered, crossed the stage road slightly above Ten Mile station.

The wagon moved on upgrade. He'd know when they topped the pass because after that it would be

136

downhill all the way to Benson's Landing on the Yellowstone. In spots Hunker would have to use brakes.

A jolting half hour dragged by and they were still going uphill. The trail got considerably rougher. Had they left the stage road?

A little farther on Rolfe was sure of it. They were still plodding uphill and now there was no trail at all. Branches scraped the wagon and Rolfe caught the smell of pine timber. The buckboard stopped and Hunker said: "Here's the key, Jody. Unlock the gate."

It was clear that they'd come to a fence with a padlocked gate in it. Hinges creaked as Jody opened it. Then they moved through it and on. A tiny riffling sound close to the right meant they were heading up the ravine of a small stream.

Presently a voice challenged from the dark. "Who's there?"

Hunker answered promptly. "It's me and Jody, Tuck. You won't need to be lonesome no more. We brung you some company."

"Light a lantern," Jody growled, "so we can see where the hell we're goin'."

Rolfe heard boots squish in mud. Tuck called out: "Foller me, Hunk. Better veer toward the hillside a bit or you'll get stuck. Dang them beavers, anyway."

In a few minutes they stopped and Hunker said, "He's all yourn, Tuck." Rolfe felt himself being lifted from the wagon bed. Two men carried him through a doorway and dropped him on a board floor. There the blindfold was taken from his eyes and the rawhide from his wrists and ankles.

A door slammed and he heard the click of a padlock. He got stiffly to his feet and began groping. After a step or two he bumped into a log wall. In inky darkness he groped around all four sides of his prison. It was a one-room log cabin with no windows.

Low voices came from outside and one of them was Hunker's. "Clint says keep him for a pet, Tuck. What for I don't know. Here's the gun we grabbed off him. It might be spotted if we took it back to town."

Jody spoke next. "Better take care of this rifle too, Tuck."

Tuck asked, "Does this jigger know where he is, Hunk?"

"How could he? He's been out like a light most of the way up here. And wrapped up like a side of beef."

With all his miseries Rolfe Kendall smiled faintly in the dark. He knew more than they thought. To reach this hideaway you turned off the Bozeman Trail somewhere between Ten Mile station and the pass. From there it was less than an hour's team walk to a padlocked gate giving to a small timbered ravine where an overflow from beaver dams muddied the approach to a windowless log cabin.

CHAPTER
TWELVE

The life of Kim Dallas hung by a thread. The vigil over him wearied Perry Hamil; it even bored him but he stuck it out. He mustn't appear to be unsympathetic in the eyes of Lucia Ripley. The army girl seemed to have adopted the boy as her personal protégé. It was gray dawn before she let herself be driven home to the fort. "I'll look in again tomorrow," she promised Doctor Monroe.

When she was gone Hamil went to his own room at the Laclede. He slept till early afternoon and then rang for a tray to be sent up. When it came a newly arrived letter lay beside the food there. The postmark was Roanoke and the writing was Diane's.

It had left Virginia seven days ago. A minimum travel time for her letters, Hamil calculated, would be one full week: two days by train; two by river boat; three by stagecoach. Hamil himself had been here ten days, so by now she must have received a copy of the Bozeman *Courier* telling of his stage adventures. For the last three days she must have wondered why she didn't get a personal account of them from Barry Rodman.

Today's letter from the girl made no mention of them. It was warmly confiding, and like the others it eagerly anticipated her own eventual journey out here. Only at the end was there a faint note of puzzlement.

Not a whisper from you, Barry dear, since your letter mailed at Miles City. But of course you couldn't write while jolting along day and night on that stage. And since getting there I suppose you've been awfully busy with the lawyers, and with affairs at the ranch. I must learn to be patient . . .

Not a shadow of suspicion — yet. And there wouldn't be, Hamil thought, if he played it right. The weekly paper would soon tell her four things about him, all linking his life to Lucia Ripley's.

Hamil burned the letter. After eating he dressed and shaved. Then Walt Mason came in with a gun at his hip and a grim worry riding his face. "Rolfe's missing, Barry. Can't locate him anywhere."

"Probably rode back to the ranch," Hamil suggested, "or to the roundup camp."

Mason shook his head. "His horse and saddle are still at the livery barn. Guess again."

"When was he last seen?"

"Checking out of the Northern Pacific Hotel at daybreak. Last night he called at the barn for his gun. McKinzie saw him just before that."

"What was he doing?"

"He was on a manhunt after the guy who sniped young Dallas." Worry deepened on the foreman's face.

"Looks like maybe he found him; and came off second best in a gunfight."

Hamil put on his hat and went with Mason to the sheriff's office. "We've inquired all over town," McKinzie reported. "Nobody heard any shooting since Kendall was last seen. We even looked in Chinatown Alley and all the dives. Only place he went in last night was the Delmonico. Nothing happened there. So he must've left town."

"On foot?"

"Not likely," the sheriff admitted. "But maybe on horseback or in a wagon. Suppose he heard something at a bar; something about missing steers or a rooftop sniping. What would he do?"

"He'd report it to you," Walt said.

"Maybe there wasn't time. Maybe the guys went out and he'd lose them if he didn't follow. If they rode away horseback he might borrow a mount from the nearest hitchrack and try to keep them in sight. If they drove away he might hide in the wagon."

"A wild guess, Sheriff."

McKinzie shrugged. "You got a better one?"

A voice spoke from the doorway. "If he hasn't. I have."

Hamil turned toward a man who was coming in. He saw a leathery rangeman, bewhiskered and past middle age. Keen gray eyes showed over the furrows of his wind-burned face.

Walt Mason greeted him. "Hi, Dad. What's new at the roundup? Barry, meet Dad Shores, wagon boss for MacAndow brothers."

The veteran gave a curt nod to Hamil, spoke grimly to McKinzie. "We've done some checking. And it gives us a new slant on those missing steers."

"Let's have it."

Shores faced Walt Mason. "Two of your crew quit in May, didn't they?"

"Right, Dad. Hickey and Yeager. In March they took money from a one-eyed halfbreed. And in May they quit."

"Two men quit *us* in May too," the MacAndow boss reported. "Ike Ranny and a man they call Hunker. Charley Anceney tells us a rider named Monte Brucker quit *his* outfit in May. Dave Fratt says Tex Orme and Joe Dakota quit him, early in May. Do you get it?"

"Like the nose on my face." Walt gave a quick nod. "Four outfits get doublecrossed in March by a man or men in their own crews. In May these doublecrossers all quit. In June the roundup shows the same kind of beef shortage in all four brands. Means it was all one big steal."

"Anceney lost sixty head," Shores reminded them. "Fratt lost ninety; you lost a hundred, Walt; and my outfit lost two hundred. Adds up to four hundred and fifty, all mature steers."

Perry Hamil wasn't too concerned about it. From his own standpoint the JR's loss of a hundred steers had a compensation. It would divert attention from his own masquerade during the next crucial weeks. He offered a half-idle question. "What's this got to do with the disappearance of Rolfe Kendall?"

142

"I dunno," Dad Shores admitted. "But I *do* know that two years ago six of those quitters were riding for Nelson Story. They brought a herd up the Bridger Trail for him. Brucker, Ranny, Dakota, Orme, Hickey and Yeager. Later he fired 'em for general cussedness. Still later one of 'em talks too much to a boy in the next cell. When the kid tries to walk across the street he gets shot. Kendall goes looking for the sniper and disappears. The way I see it, it's all one big package. Find out what happened to those steers and you'll find out what happened to Kendall."

Walt Mason had the glimmer of an idea. "Look, Sheriff. We thought maybe the JR steers were butchered and the beef peddled to agencies and settlements. They might do that with a hundred head, but not with four or five times that many. They'd draw too much attention. Especially in the spring when the stuff's not fat. Folks would wonder why they didn't hold 'em till fall. So it's likely they didn't butcher 'em at all."

"You think they're holding them in some pocket of the hills?"

"Either that," Walt concluded, "or they shipped 'em to market by rail."

"The end of the North Pacific rails was more than four hundred miles east, in Dakota. A drive to that railhead would have to go down the Yellowstone to its mouth, then down the Missouri into Dakota. "A drive on that trail would be noticed and reported," McKinzie argued. "Stage drivers and freighters and wagon trains would pass it day after day. I don't think they'd risk going that way, Walt."

143

"Neither do I," Mason agreed. "But what about the Utah Northern, in Idaho?"

McKinzie and Shores exchanged glances, each nodding thoughtfully. Until a year ago the nearest railhead to the south had been Corrine, Utah, on the main line of the Union Pacific. But in recent months a branch line called the Utah Northern had been pushing up from Corrine into Idaho.

"They've laid track as far as Idaho Falls," McKinzie said. "If those steers were shipped by rail, I'll bet they were loaded at Idaho Falls."

"They could go straight through to Omaha," Shores admitted, "by way of Corrine and Cheyenne."

The sheriff reached for pad and pencil. "I'll telegraph the Idaho Falls sheriff. He can check with the Utah Northern agent there and find out if about fifteen carloads of steers were shipped out in April or May; and if so who was the shipper?"

The telegram would have to go by a long, round-about route, east to Omaha, then west to Utah, then north along the new branch line to Idaho Falls.

While they discussed it Hamil saw Lucia Ripley drive by in a Fort Ellis rig. He caught up with her at a hitchrack. As he tied her buggy horse she asked anxiously, "How is Kim?"

"I was just on my way to find out," Hamil said glibly. He gave her his arm and they went up narrow stairs to the office and makeshift hospital operated by Doctor Monroe.

Monroe met them in the hallway and the look on his tired face wasn't encouraging. "I've drugged him to

144

sleep, Lucia. You can't see him today. Maybe tomorrow if he hangs on that long."

"Is it *that* bad?" Hamil asked.

"It's always that bad, Mr. Rodman, when a bullet goes in one side of you and comes out the other. Best I can say for him right now is that there's no infection."

"Isn't there anything we can do?" the army girl asked earnestly.

Monroe gave her a pat on the shoulder. "You did plenty last night, young lady, when you passed a hat out on the walk. You fattened up the hospital fund a lot."

"But it was for Kim's doctor's bill," Lucia said.

"There won't be any doctor's bill," Monroe told her. "Now run along, both of you."

Hamil took Lucia over to the Laclede for tea and cakes. "Where's Walt?" she asked him.

"Busy playing detective." Hamil relayed to her the latest about the missing steers. "On top of that, we can't find Rolfe Kendall."

The mysteries of a missing cowboy and missing cattle kept them in intimate talk there. And to those who looked on, and especially to Editor Alderson who came in for a cup of coffee, it seemed like a vivid exchange of confidences. Hamil wanted it that way. The *Courier* had a social gossip column which was sure to be read by a girl in Virginia.

They went out to Lucia's rig and Hamil persuaded her to wait while he got his own horse from the livery barn. Then he rode at her wheel as she drove east out of town.

The late afternoon sun caught brilliant glints from her hair and Hamil, as she said goodbye to him at the sentry gate, realized that she was more than beautiful. Concern for the boy, Kim, had brought new and lovely depths of sympathy to her eyes; just as excitement over the Kendall mystery brightened the delicate pink of her cheeks. "If you find him let me know right away, Barry."

"I'll come loping straight out here, Lucia." With a gallant wave of his flat, black hat, Perry Hamil wheeled his mount and rode back to town.

A new temptation whispered. "Why not? She likes me. So why not?"

Till now he'd been merely using the girl as a pawn with which to shake off an entanglement in Virginia. He'd planned only to hang around long enough to get his hands on an estate; then off to some far land with the spoils. But now . . . "Why not? She likes me. And dammit, I like her too."

He rode on with a dream building in his brain. A dream of Perry Hamil, outlaw killer from Texas, settling down with Lucia as master and mistress of the JR ranch.

His sense of exhilaration came to an end during supper at the Laclede. Ridley Davis and Walt Mason were sharing a table with him, the lawyer bubbling with questions. No answer to the sheriff's telegram was expected till tomorrow. "I'll wager you didn't expect to run into anything like this, Barry. A regular Wild West show! So you think they shipped the cattle by rail, do you, Walt?"

"Damn the cattle!" Walt brooded. "What worries me is Rolfe Kendall. I sure took a shine to that fella."

146

"What's got the whole town standing on its head," Davis went on, "is this 'rich and influential' backer Yeager mentioned in the jail. Who the dickens can he be?"

"Yeh, who can he be?" Mason's eyes fixed narrowly on a table at the rear. "If Yeager had said 'rich and crooked,' I'd say there he sits right now."

Hamil looked that way and saw two men who'd just come in. One was short and wide; the other lean and tall. One was Chips Charny of the Delmonico; the other was his new lookout, Harry De Shon.

De Shon was staring this way and his stare met Hamil's. The man's eyes narrowed. Then he turned to his employer, leaned across the table to speak in a low, guarded voice.

It spoiled Hamil's appetite and changed his plans. He'd intended to stay in town a few days and build himself up with Lucia. Now all he could think of was getting out of sight from that accursed De Shon.

Abruptly he decided to ride back to the ranch. There was nothing to stop him. As master of the JR he could come and go as he pleased.

Mason didn't go with him. Perry Hamil was alone when he rode into the ranch yard the next afternoon. He found Pony Willard filling a horse trough at the well. "Did Walt go back to the roundup?" Pony asked.

Hamil shook his head. "Rolfe Kendall took off somewhere. Walt's staying in town to find out where and why."

At the kitchen the Chinese cook served him a fresh-baked meat pie. "Anybody been around, Charley?"

"One day Mr. Mike is here to see you."

"Mike Lockhart? He wants to buy me out, Charley. Wonder why he's in such an all-fired hurry!"

Later Hamil changed to corduroys and buckled on a gun belt. He went to his shed wall target and began shooting. The shots brought Pony Willard limping up. The choreman squinted critically at the newest bullet holes.

Today all were on the cardboard and three were only a few inches off the bull's-eye. "You're gettin' some better, boss."

Hamil smiled covertly. He wondered what Pony would think if he knew what the man calling himself Barry Rodman could really do with a gun. The trick was to improve slowly so that it would look like a newly acquired skill.

A day would come, maybe sooner than he expected; when Barry Rodman would need to use that skill. What with a hunt for a missing man and missing cattle, gunfights were breeding in Gallatin Valley. The master of the JR might be in the thick of them. Any day he might need to draw against a fast gunman; maybe against someone like Harry De Shon.

And when Barry Rodman downed his man, no one must be surprised or suspicious.

The next day Hamil practiced both morning and evening. He let his hits creep closer and closer to the bull's-eye.

He kept it up for still another day, often with the choreman standing by. "You're sure ketchin' on quick," Pony marveled. "For a tenderfoot, it's the closest shootin' I ever seen."

"Thanks, Pony. Walt talks like he's expecting trouble. So I want to be ready when it comes."

The choreman freshened his quid and pondered. After watching a few more shots he offered advice. "Close shootin' won't be enough, boss, in a showdown with real gunnies. It'll take *fast* shootin', too. Why don't you try shootin' from a draw?"

"A good idea, Pony." Hamil holstered his gun. Then he made a slow draw and fired. His next draw wasn't quite so slow. He kept at it, and his tenth draw was almost fast.

Pony limped over to the henhouse where the cook was gathering eggs. "Never seen anything like it, Charley, the way he ketches on. Made three bull's-eyes just now, out of ten shots. Let fly from a snatch draw each time. Little more practice and he can match slugs with the best of 'em."

At sundown Walt Mason rode in from Bozeman. As he unsaddled Pony Willard told again about the target practice. "He's gettin' to be an A-one gun hand, Walt."

"He'll need to be," the foreman said grimly, "if he rides along where I'm going. I'll take a daybreak start, Pony. Be gone a week or two, maybe. When Mack Boyd comes in from the roundup, tell him to take over here."

At supper Mason explained it to his employer. "We got an answer from Idaho Falls, Barry. That's about two hundred miles south of here. The Utah Northern agent there says twelve carloads of big steers were shipped out late in May, billed to the stockyards at Omaha. At thirty-five steers to the car, it would make four hundred and twenty head. Figures about right. In April or May they'd lose about thirty on the way. A few weaklings would die and a few more would stray off at night. The rustlers wouldn't dare take time to hunt for them."

"Who shipped the cattle?" Hamil asked.

"They were billed out by the Targhee Cattle Company. No outfit by that name belongs to the Idaho Stockgrowers' Association. So it looks like just a blind to cover up a beef-stealing operation."

"How much did the shipment bring?"

"Fourteen thousand net, after deducting freight charges and commission. One man rode the caboose of the cattle train, calling himself Lou Harrison, secretary-treasurer of the Targhee Cattle Co. He collected the check, cashed it in Omaha, and no one knows where he is now."

"It's just a cover name, this Lou Harrison?"

"McKinzie thinks so. The only lead we've got is the word Targhee. There's a Targhee Pass a hundred miles south of here, a little way into Idaho. It's on the Continental Divide, but only seven thousand feet high. You could push cattle over it in late spring if you didn't mind losing a few head. Just beyond it you come to Henry's Lake, which is about twenty-five miles west of Yellowstone Park."

"Which adds up to what?"

"We had a talk with Russ Sullivan who tends bar at Sackett's saloon. Russ once proved up on a homestead near Henry's Lake. We asked him if he ever heard of the Targhee Cattle Company. He said yes, he dug post holes one time for an outfit that was stringing barbed wire around twelve sections of land, about halfway between Targhee Pass and the lake. It made an eight-thousand-acre pasture, three miles wide by four long, mostly timber, but with plenty of good grass. Russ says they paid him with a check signed Targhee Cattle Co."

"On what bank?"

"He can't remember what bank. It was two years ago. The check was good. Russ cashed it right here in Bozeman."

"So you're riding south?"

"At the crack of dawn. A posse'll be waiting at the Gallatin Gateway. Want to come along?"

"I'll think it over," Hamil said. "Anything new about Kendall?"

"Not that you could put a finger on. But I'm playin' a hunch, Barry. Had lunch with Lucia Ripley and she thinks I'm right."

His hunch, Mason explained, was that the hideaway mentioned by Dutch Yeager was the twelve-section fenced ranch beyond Targhee Pass, and that riders who'd driven the stolen steers to Idaho Falls were holed up there now. "It's about halfway," the foreman said. "They could rest the cattle a couple of weeks in that pasture. No more mountains beyond there, and good feed all the way, so they'd get the steers to the cars in fair flesh. Once they were shipped, I figure the riders would go back to the hideaway ranch and lie low."

"And Rolfe Kendall?"

"Could have got wind of it and been knocked on the head. Since we can't find his body they must've hauled him away. Maybe for a chip to trade with in case they get cornered."

"You think they could be holding him at the Targhee ranch?"

"There's a one-to-ten chance of it. Lucia Ripley's all fired up about it. She wants us to burn leather that way plenty fast."

When it was put like that, Hamil didn't see how he could stay behind. It was more than an expedition to run down rustlers; in Lucia's mind at least it was a rescue party out to save Rolfe Kendall's life. Hamil had a feeling he'd lose ground with her if he didn't join up.

"Count me in, Walt. Lucky I've been learning how to shoot a gun. Looks like I'll get a chance to use it."

"It sure does," Mason agreed. "Finding Rolfe there's a long shot. But you can bet your boots *someone*'ll be there. Maybe Lou Harrison himself. Him and a crew of gunnies. Betcha I can name four of 'em right now."

"Which four?"

"Four who quit good jobs early in May and haven't been seen since. Monte Brucker, a guy named Dakota, Ike Ranny and Tex Orme."

What part of Texas, Hamil wondered uneasily, had Tex Orme come from? "Any of those men got records?"

"Orme has. He killed a man at Rawlins one time; pleaded self-defense and got acquitted." A grim smile curved Walt's lips. "So if you see this fella Orme, see him first; and shoot fast."

"I'll do my best," Hamil promised.

An afterthought made Mason bring a letter from his pocket. "For you, Barry. It came in on yesterday's stage."

Hamil took it to his room, read through it from end to end.

. . . Thank goodness you arrived safely, dear. I've just read about it in the Bozeman paper. Now I know why I haven't had any letters. The stage bringing them probably tipped over, like yours did, and your letters to me are all floating sadly down the Yellowstone River. It's a wonder you weren't drowned, Barry dear. Instead you were a hero and carried the lovely redhead safely to shore. Is she really beautiful? If I didn't know you so well, I'd be terribly jealous . . .

On the surface it was gay and trusting. But Hamil, after a second reading, sensed a note of restraint. She was beginning to wonder about Lucia Ripley.

CHAPTER
THIRTEEN

In the morning he rode with Walt to Gallatin Gateway, striking the river just above Zeke Sales' sawmill. A six-man posse was waiting there. Each man had an extra horse; and Indian Jake, a friendly Crow who worked as a roustabout for the Anceney outfit, followed with a pack mare loaded with grub. McKinzie wasn't there but he'd sent along a deputy named Jim Wilder.

"Just to make it legal," Wilder said, "an Idaho deputy'll meet us at the territory line. He'll have a batch of John Doe warrants. Let's ride."

They trailed up the West Gallatin and soon passed the mouth of Spanish Creek. At noon each man changed to a fresh horse. Night caught them near Blackmore's cabin in West Gallatin canyon. As they made camp someone noticed that Hamil's saddle was the only one that didn't have a scabbard with a rifle in it.

"I wouldn't know how to use one," Hamil explained.

"But he's getting handy with a short gun," Walt said.

Two of the posse were from Anceney's outfit, two from MacAndow brothers and one from the Fratt ranch. When the Idaho deputy joined them they'd be a force of nine men.

Wilder had them moving at sunup. Before noon they came out into a grassy plateau basin. They pushed on across the basin, past Big Spring where a small herd of elk were feeding. Always the clear snowfed waters of the West Gallatin led them up and on.

Beyond the basin was another narrow canyon and at the top of this a divide with patches of snow not yet quite melted. They'd come forty miles since sunup and Hamil dismounted stiffly. "You think the thieves passed this way?"

"It's the shortest way," Mason answered, "to Henry's Lake and Idaho Falls."

"I've counted five beef carcasses," the Fratt rider said, "in the last three miles. Just what you'd expect, pushin' stuff through here early in May."

They camped on the Divide and in the morning rode down into the watershed of the upper Madison. To the east the jagged Absarokas made a snowy wall across Yellowstone Park. Lodgepole pine closed in to shut the peaks from sight. The posse pressed on and soon was fording the broad swift riffles of the Madison.

"Where does this river go?" Hamil asked.

"The Madison, the Gallatin and the Jefferson," Mason told him, "all come together to make the Missouri, about thirty miles below Bozeman."

"Howcome they gave 'em those names?" he asked.

"That's an easy one," Walt said. "Who explored this range in the first place? Couple of guys named Lewis and Clark. Who was president then? Tom Jefferson.

Who were the two top rods in his cabinet? Couple of guys named Madison and Gallatin."

They slogged out of the river, wet to the stirrups. Hamil saw a she-bear with two cubs lumber off through the forest. "We've got one more hump to get over," Wilder said as the trail slanted upward again.

Targhee Pass was the Idaho line and on it a slim young deputy was waiting. Wilder had had dealings with him before. "Boys, this is Dave Crago. From here on he'll give the orders."

Crago led them on and down. The sun was low when he picked a camp on a small creek feeding Henry's Fork of the Snake. "Jake," Wilder said to the Crow Indian cook, "dip up some of this Pacific Ocean water and make some coffee with it."

"We can strike that pasture before noon tomorrow," Crago told them. "I've ridden by there a couple of times. Never could see anything wrong with it."

"Is it an operating ranch?"

"Didn't see any cattle. Only a few riding horses. Nobody there but a caretaker. I figured some land speculator bought up the acreage, fenced it, and is holding it for a land boom."

"When were you there last, Dave?"

"Not since fall. But when we got McKinzie's wire I checked the records. Title to one quarter section, where the house stands, is in the name of Lou Harrison. The rest of it's government land, under lease to the Targhee Cattle Company."

Indian Jake had bacon sizzling when Hamil rolled out of his blankets. And soon after sunrise they were riding southwest toward Henry's Lake. The lake was like a big silver mirror with a belt of open grass surrounding it and slanting upward to the wooded hills.

"Veer to the right here," Crago said, "and keep to the edge of the trees."

A four-wire fence stopped them. It cornered just outside the trees. "The only gate I know of," Crago said, "is out in the open and they can see it from the house. So we better cut the fence right here. Maybe we can surprise them, that way."

The Fratt hand took pliers from his saddle and cut the wires. After riding through the gap they used one of the cut wires to patch the other three. "If they've got stolen stock in this pasture," Walt said, "we better keep it corraled for evidence."

This piny, mountainside pasture, four miles long and three wide, looked to Hamil like a perfect place to hide cattle and men.

The house, which came in sight sooner than Hamil expected, was only a little way back in the trees. A half mile directly in front of it was a plank gate. "Do they keep a padlock on it?" Wilder asked.

"Not when I stopped by last fall," Crago said. "But they can sure spot you from the house while you're still rifle range away."

It was a stout log house, the kind that could stop bullets. A shed and corral were back of it. The corral had two horses in it.

"Two men won't fight nine," Crago decided. "So let's go."

They rode toward the house, nine abreast. This east side of it had only one window. Mason rode with a hand on the stock of his rifle.

There was no challenge. But Hamil heard someone stirring inside. He saw a face at the window, staring out. The man would see nine armed men two of whom had deputy badges. Crago was right. Two men would hardly fight nine.

The face disappeared. "Three of you cover that window," Crago ordered. "Rest of us'll take the front."

The front had a door and two windows. The door opened and an unarmed man came out. He had shifty eyes and a plump, stubbled face. The eyes blinked when an Anceney cowboy called him by name. "Hi, Monte. Where've you been since April? We missed you at the roundup."

Wilder shot a question. "Who else is in there, Brucker?"

"Nobody but the cook," Monte Brucker said.

Inside they found only one man. None of the posse had ever seen him before. He gave his name as Nash and said he'd been hired as a cook, only two weeks ago. He stood tight-lipped and sullen with his back to a wall as Wilder fired questions.

"Where's Lou Harrison? What about Ranny and Orme and Dakota?"

Brucker's frightened look changed to one of sly caution. "Lou Harrison? Who's he? Never heard of him. Ain't seen Ike or Tex or Dakota since I left Bozeman."

158

"You claim you didn't help 'em drive steers to the railroad?"

"What steers? All I did was come over here to look for a job. Man named Smith hired me as caretaker here. He sent a cook out, but I ain't seen anyone else."

That was Monte's story and he stuck to it. No one believed him. Nash looked more like a hard-bitten outlaw than a cook. His bunk had a gunbelt hanging by it and two rifles stood in a corner. "They wouldn't send a cook out here to cook for just one man," Walt argued. "Where's the rest of 'em?"

"There's only me and the cook," Brucker insisted.

The house had four rooms and bunks for ten men. A freshly butchered side of beef hung on the back porch. A larder was stocked with staple foods. A long table had chairs and boxes lining it. A dozen men could be fed here.

Mason picked up a beer check issued at a place called the Targhee Tavern. "It's a crossroads saloon," Crago said, "about fifteen miles southeast of here. Might be the gang's there right now."

It was Wilder who found the first real clew. Among scraps in a table drawer he came across a receipt issued by the Laclede Hotel in Bozeman. It was for a month's rent of a room and made out to Clinton Bowers.

Mason pounced on it. "Wow! Now we're making hay! I know this Clinton Bowers. He's a cattle speculator who's been staying at the Laclede, off and on, for the last year. When a drove of cattle comes through town, he bids on it. Sometimes he rides around the county ranches to look at fat steers. He made a bid at the JR, one time."

"He showed up at the Hat, one day," the Fratt rider remembered. A hat on the left ribs was Dave Fratt's brand. "He bid on a bunch of he-stuff. But it was a penny under the market and Dave turned him down."

Mason's eyes narrowed. "Come to think of it, he bid a penny low at the JR too. When I look back, this Bowers was always bidding on cattle but I can't remember he ever bought any. How about you, Hank?"

"Check," the Anceney rider said.

It was the same with the other Gallatin County men. They'd all known the speculator to bid on cattle, but never high enough to make a buy.

"So he's a phony," Walt Mason concluded. "Pretending to be a beef buyer gave him a chance to ride around the ranches. He could look the stuff over and pick out his next steal. With a spy on each big ranch, the rest was easy. Most of the time he'd sit in the Laclede lobby smokin' two-bit cigars."

"He dropped a five-dollar bill in my hat," Perry Hamil remembered, "when Lucia Ripley took a collection for Kim Dallas, the night Kim was shot."

Wilder gave a shrewd nod. "He's a slick one, all right. Anybody who thinks Lou Harrison and Clint Bowers aren't one and the same man, go to the foot of the class. Less than a week ago I saw him myself with a posy in his buttonhole, breasting the Laclede bar."

"With fourteen thousand dollars steer money in his wallet," Walt put in.

"What," Crago asked, "does he look like?"

160

"Medium build, middle age, with a wine-red face. Dresses like a big town banker. Has thick curly hair and parts it in the middle."

"Then what are we waiting for? Why not ride back to Bozeman and pick him up?"

"We'd better pick up his crew first," Wilder thought. "Chances are they're off on a drinking bout somewhere. Let's hole up here overnight and lay for 'em. When they come riding home we'll pop it to 'em."

Wilder, Crago, Mason and Hamil went outside to talk it over. In a little while Wilder called the others out and announced the decision. "Buck, tie Brucker and Nash up and keep an eye on them. Walt, pick three men and patrol the pasture. Each can take a fourth of it. Look for two things: cattle sign showing that four hundred head were held here lately; and maybe a fat beef or two they left here on purpose when they drove the herd south. Meat for the crew till the next operation."

The last idea made sense, Hamil thought. That fresh side of beef on the back porch lent support to it.

Walt picked his three men. One of them was Hamil himself. The rest of the posse took rifles to watch alertly from the front windows. "Not likely those birds'll show up before dark," Crago said. "But we've got to be ready."

Mason and his three men stepped into saddles. All other horses were put out of sight in the shed. "Barry," Walt directed, "you take the pasture's northwest quarter. I'll take the northeast. You other two men can divide the south half between you."

161

They separated and rode in four directions. Hamil, angling up a gentle slope, passed from scrub pine into juniper and then into pine again. Droppings and trampled grass soon convinced him that a sizable bunch of cattle had recently been held here. Solid proof would come only if they found a living steer with a Montana brand on it.

Hamil pressed on through the timber and saw no life but a covey of grouse. The west fence stopped him. He followed it uphill to the northwest corner. Here he was high on the mountainside in rough, rocky going.

Turning east along the north fence he rode till a patch of juniper brush made him detour downhill. The detour brought him into an open park on a bench. Last year's cured grass on the bench was knee high; and on the far side of it Hamil saw a grazing steer.

He jogged that way to read the brand. The steer was a three-year-old, unusually fat for June. Just the kind a hideaway crew might hold out for meat. The brand was U Bar. Walt had coached him on the main Gallatin Valley brands. U Bar was the mark used by MacAndow brothers.

Hamil smiled and tipped his hat to the steer. "Thanks, fella. You're boostin' my stock a lot. For turning you up I'll be the fair-haired boy with Walt Mason and all the rest of the Bozeman bozos. Not to mention . . ."

He broke off and his smile faded. A rider had come out of the trees and was loping toward him. Not one of the Wilder posse; so he was bound to be one of the hideaway crew. The man wore a gray range hat with the brim turned up in front. A gun was holstered at his hip and he rode with a hand on its grip.

He reined up a length away from Hamil. His eyes stared a challenge and his hand was still on the gun. "Who the hell are you, mister? This here's private property. Start movin' before I . . ."

A strange and sudden change came over the man. All at once he was no longer hostile and his lips parted in a grin. "Danged if it ain't Perry Hamil! Golly Moses! How's things down at Laredo, Perry?"

"Wild and woolly, same as always." Hamil gave the answer cautiously, while his wits groped for the right move. This, of course, would be Tex Orme. There'd been a flock of tinhorn toughies on the lower Rio Grande, three years ago, when Perry Hamil was at the peak of his notorious career there. Lesser outlaws had fawned on him, and he couldn't remember them all. But they would know Perry Hamil, naturally, as serfs would know a king.

Orme was entirely relaxed now. His hand left the gun butt and he began rolling a cigaret. "When did Clint take you on, Perry? He promised he'd send a replacement for Roy Hickey. But golly Moses, we never figured we'd get a top gun like you. Did you stop by the house and see Brucker?"

"Yes." Hamil's single word had a flat sound and something in the tone must have warned Orme. A cagey alertness came into his eyes.

And for Perry Hamil there was only one way out. He didn't dare deliver Orme to the posse at the point of a gun. For when they began calling him Barry Rodman,

163

Orme would start laughing. He'd tell tales on Hamil. Tales which would blast away all hope of inheriting the Rodman estate and in the end send Hamil in shackles back to a Texas gallows.

The hard decision in Hamil's eyes again warned Orme. He dropped the half-rolled smoke and went for his gun.

He got it out of the holster but his finger went dead on the trigger. A bullet from a faster man drilled through his heart. Tex Orme was pitching from the saddle when Hamil fired again. But at the second trigger pull Hamil aimed high, missing on purpose.

Dismounting, Hamil knelt beside Orme to make sure he was dead. The gun in the man's hand hadn't been fired. Perry Hamil took a bullet from it; then he took one of two empty shells from his own forty-five. The unfired cartridge from Orme's gun went into his own cylinder, and the empty went into Orme's.

Hamil twirled the cylinders to put the traded bullets in the right places. He left Orme's gun under the man's outstretched right hand.

Then Walt Mason came spurring from the trees. "What's up, Barry?"

Hamil nodded toward a steer with a U Bar on its flank; then toward a dead man who lay by a riderless horse. "Who is he, Walt?"

Mason dismounted, turned the body face up. "He's one of the two men who quit the Hat outfit, in early May. Orme's his name. Chain lightning with a gun, I've heard. Gosh! It's a wonder he didn't blow your head off, Barry."

164

Hamil grimaced. "He tried to, but I was lucky. He rode up and asked what the hell I was doing here. I said I was looking for stolen steers. My luck was that his horse shied just as he drew and fired. It made him miss and gave me time to get off a shot myself."

Mason picked up Orme's gun and saw the empty shell in it. A frank admiration lighted his eyes as they met Hamil's. "Call it luck if you want to, Barry. It took nerve, too, and plenty of it. Your Uncle John would have been proud of you, fella. I'll sit on the evidence while you ride to the house and tell Wilder."

CHAPTER
FOURTEEN

Early in the morning three men went out through the pasture gate and rode southeast toward Targhee Tavern. The rest of the posse, with Crago in command, remained in alert ambush at the hideaway ranch house in case others of the Lou Harrison crew came home.

However, the absentees might be indulging themselves at the nearest trailside bar. "Ike Ranny and Dakota, to name two of them," Walt Mason said. He was riding stirrup to stirrup between Deputy Wilder and a Hat hand named Chuck Ward.

"Ought to be half a dozen of 'em, somewhere," Wilder estimated. "We'd better scout that tavern and count saddles, before we bust in on em."

They angled across an open valley and forded Henry's Fork of the Snake. Beyond it they struck a main trail pointing south toward Blackfoot and Idaho Falls. "This is the way our beef went," Chuck Ward muttered, "on the way to the cars. I'd sure like to draw a bead on those bozos."

"Speaking of beads," Wilder remarked, "that tenderfoot from Virginia drew a pretty good one on Tex Orme. Where the heck did he learn to shoot like that?"

"He's been flippin' slug at a bull's-eye," Mason explained, "ever since he hit the JR. At first he couldn't shoot worth a cent. But look at him now!"

At the far edge of the valley, where timber began again, they sighted an unpainted plank house with sheds behind it. "That's Targhee Tavern," Wilder said. "Accordin' to Crago, a German couple by the name of Shultz run it."

"They've got two customers." Walt pointed to a pair of saddled horses at the front hitchrail.

"There could be more in the shed," Wilder warned. "Let's circle to the timber and come at 'em from the other side."

They veered to the timber and let it screen their approach to the sheds. Chuck Ward dismounted for a look. "Only one bronc," he reported. "It's a brand I never saw before."

"When Ranny and Dakota were last seen, what horses were they riding?"

"Wyoming brands, I think," Chuck remembered. "Dakota had a blaze-faced sorrel."

"I'll go in at the back door," Wilder decided. "Walt, you and Chuck take the front."

Mason and Ward circled to the front hitchrail. Of the two saddled horses already tied there, one was a blazefaced sorrel.

"Your old bunkie at the Hat," Walt said grimly. They dismounted, tied their mounts at the rail, then moved to the open front door and looked in. It was a big, barny barroom with a rough plank floor and walls. The bar, tables and chairs had been made by amateur carpenters, mostly out of slash lumber with bark on one side. Everything was cheap and crudely made; yet the floor and windows had a fresh-scrubbed look.

A fat man behind the bar was probably Shultz. He was pushing two schooners of beer toward customers. One of the customers was a stranger to Walt. The other was a cowboy he'd known as Dakota, late of the Fratt ranch crew.

They didn't see Mason and Ward, because Deputy Wilder was coming in at the back door. They were looking at his badge and at his leveled gun. "Put 'em up, everybody. You're under arrest. Walt, better see if Fatty's got a shotgun back there."

Walt walked in with Ward at his heels. The surprise was complete and there was no resistance. Dakota backed away from the bar with his hands up. The other customer did the same. "You got a warrant?" Dakota demanded sullenly.

His companion showed a better temper. He wore leather gauntlets and had the swarthiness of a Spaniard. "You are mistake," he insisted with a tolerant smile. "I am only a traveler who stops for the night here."

"If you can prove it," Wilder promised, "you can keep on traveling. Find anything, Walt?"

Walt was now back of the bar where he found no shotgun or weapon of any kind. "I am Herman Shultz and I am an honest man," the proprietor pleaded. To Walt he seemed neither guilty nor frightened, only offended at having been misjudged.

"Likely he's right," Wilder admitted. "Crago says he usta run a hotel at Hailey and had a good reputation there. Where's your wife, Shultz?"

"For a week now she visits her sister in Blackfoot," Shultz told them.

Wilder advanced to disarm and search the two customers. There was nothing on either to connect them with stolen cattle, or with the hideaway ranch.

The swarthy man gave his name as Romero. He was traveling north from Utah, he said, hoping to find work in Montana. "Dark overtakes me here," he explained with a smooth smile, "so I stay all night."

"Then why didn't you ride on north, first thing this, morning?" It was now past ten o'clock.

"My horse needs a rest. Go look in the shed, señor, and you will see he has come a long way."

"What about that, Shultz? Is he on the level?"

"I know nothing of him," Shultz said, "except that he came at dark yesterday. He was alone and asked for lodging."

The deputy turned back to Dakota. "Where's Ike Ranny?"

"Haven't seen Ranny since I left Montana."

"How about Brucker and Orme?"

"Haven't seen them, neither. You got nothing on me; not a danged thing."

Wilder and Mason exchanged glances. Both knew it was true. Dakota had a perfect right to be at this public bar. Brucker could probably be convicted because he'd been found at the hideaway ranch along with Orme and a stolen steer. But not Dakota.

"You know a sharper named Lou Harrison?" Wilder asked Shultz.

"I never met him," the German said. "But I have heard that a man of that name owns land near here."

Walt broke in impatiently. "What about two saddled horses at the rack? One belongs to Dakota. The other one can't be Romero's, because his is in a shed."

Shultz said: "I don't think it is Otto's; he isn't up yet."

"Otto who?"

"Otto is the only name he gives me. He is asleep upstairs."

A wall ladder led to an open trap in the ceiling. Obviously there was a loft bunkroom. "Who else," Wilder demanded, "is up there?"

"Only Otto," Shultz insisted.

Walt looked sharply at Dakota. "You and Otto were about to hit for the hideaway? So you saddled his horse for him?"

Dakota had a cornered look. He didn't answer. "Keep 'em covered, Chuck," Wilder said, "while Walt and I take a look in the loft."

The guns of Dakota and Romero were in his hand. He laid them on the bar near Chuck Ward's elbow. Being the only armed man in it, Chuck had complete command of the room.

Wilder shinnied up the ladder and Walt followed. They came out in a bare-floored loft with six canvas cots in it. Three of the cots were neatly made. The other three had been slept in. Except for Wilder and Mason, no one was in the loft now.

Wilder moved from one to another of the three slept-in cots, feeling the blankets of each. "Two cold and one warm," he reported. "Which means Otto hasn't been up more than ten minutes or so."

The loft's one window was open. A lariat, tied to a wall hook, hung out of it. "He heard us raid the bar," Walt concluded. "So he flew the coop."

Before Wilder could answer, a gun roared below. It seemed to come from the barroom's front door. Walt heard a groan of pain as someone fell to the floor. Then a scamper of feet. He ran toward the trap but Wilder beat him to it. The deputy started down the ladder but was only halfway through it when a second shot boomed from the barroom entrance. "I'm hit, Walt! Stop 'em!" As Wilder gasped out the last word he lost his grip and fell twelve feet to the floor below.

Walt Mason wasted a precious half minute as he began lowering himself through the trap. Then his brain got in gear and he knew better than to go legs-first down that ladder. His legs and his body would be an easy target before his eyes could even see who was down there.

Instead, Walt ran to the loft window. He scrambled through it, his left hand with a grip on the hanging rope. With his right hand holding a forty-five gun he slid hard and fast to a bumping stop on the ground.

On this south side of the building no one was in sight. But Walt heard hoof sounds as mounted men moved off north from the hitchrack. He picked himself up and raced to the front corner. Rounding it he saw three horsemen making off at a lope, one of them leading a saddled mount. The rack was empty. The man who led the extra horse twisted in his saddle to look back. Walt glimpsed his face and knew him. Ike Ranny! Otto was merely a name Ranny had used to fool Shultz.

In a boiling rage Walt chased them with bullets. Five times he hipped his trigger. They were desperation shots, fired at a range too long for short-gun shooting.

But one of the five shots was a hit. Two of the outlaws kept racing on, and one of them swayed from the saddle. He fell sideways and for a moment hung head down. His foot caught in a stirrup and he was dragged for a jump or two. Then the boot came free and he lay motionless in the trail. The horse continued on. The man who called himself Romero snatched its bridle rein, leading it far and fast beyond the reach of Walt Mason.

A smothering humiliation weighed on Walt. He stood by the hitchrack, seething impotently as he reloaded his gun. The man he'd shot from the saddle didn't move. By the brownness of his jacket Walt knew he was Dakota.

Then Walt Mason went inside and saw Wilder pick himself up from the floor. The deputy staggered groggily to a chair and sat down. He had a bloody leg and a bump on his head.

Two guns which Wilder had laid on the bar weren't there now. And Chuck Ward of the Hat ranch lay still on the floor. "How bad is he hit, Walt?"

Mason kneeled beside Ward and knew at once that he'd never ride again. "It's a head hit. He's dead."

The bloodless, frightened face of Shultz appeared above the bar. "It was Otto," he reported hoarsely. "Otto came to the front door and shot him down."

"You've got the name wrong," Walt said bitterly. "He's Ike Ranny. Tear up a sheet and bind Wilder's leg."

It was only a flesh wound. "What hurts is the bump on my noggin. The floor hit me a heap harder than the bullet did. Did they leave us afoot, Walt?"

"Not quite. Romero left a horse in the shed. That guy sure had me fooled."

"Me too," Wilder admitted.

"So now I'll have to grab his horse and race them to Bozeman."

The deputy's stare showed that his wits weren't quite clear yet. "Bozeman?"

"That's where they're heading, on a bet," Walt said. "If they beat me there they'll warn Clint Bowers. Then Clint'll gather up his money, check out of the Laclede and get clean away."

Wilder saw it and gave a grim nod. "It's better'n a hundred miles, Walt. But you're right. If they beat you to Bozeman we'll lose Bowers."

A telegram to McKinzie, they agreed, would take too long. A rider would have to take it, to a distant army post; from there it would have to go by military wire to Idaho Falls, from there by a series of roundabout railroad wires via Utah, Omaha and St. Paul.

"They're two men with four horses, Walt," Wilder warned. "If you try to pass 'em in that canyon they'll gun hell out of you."

"Maybe I can slip by 'em at night," Walt said. "Shultz, fix up a grub pack for me while I go saddle that horse."

CHAPTER
FIFTEEN

Riding Romero's horse, Walt made Targhee Pass by mid-afternoon. Signs told him that two mounted men, leading two extra horses, were still ahead of him. Proof came just north of the pass when he met a strayman from a Henry's Fork ranch.

"Yep," the cowboy said. " 'Bout an hour ago I passed a party like that at the Madison River ford. They was headin' north."

Walt rode on, sparing his horse. He didn't want to catch up with Ranny and Romero until well after dark, when they should be asleep in camp. Meantime he wasn't much worried about Wilder. At the tavern he'd made the deputy comfortable. And Crago, at the hideaway ranch, by now would be sending out scouts to see why Wilder, Mason and Ward didn't report back.

Just before sunset Walt crossed the Madison and rested briefly on the north bank. A patch of cured grass there made feed for his horse. He rode on, then, along a trail sloping gently upward through lodgepole pine.

Before midnight his mount began playing out. The grade was still rising. The men ahead each had a remount. They could switch from saddle to saddle every few miles. Would they ride all night?

If they did, Walt knew they'd beat him to Bozeman. They'd warn Clint Bowers — and who else? How big was the crowd around Bowers? Was steer-stealing its only operation? Someone in it had sniped Kim Dallas — and that someone couldn't have been anybody at the Idaho hideaway. So Bowers was bound to have other gunmen at his call, either in or near Bozeman.

The flare of a campfire showed through trees ahead. Walt dismounted, led his horse as he moved on cautiously afoot. If the campers were Ranny and the Spaniard, he must pass them in the dark and be ten miles ahead by dawn.

With this purpose he left the trail and veered into the pines. Treading softly, Walt was almost past the camp on a wide detour when he heard the bark of a dog. So the camp wasn't Ranny's. Nor was it Ranny's voice which challenged from the dark. "Who's out there?"

"Member of a sheriff's posse," Walt shouted. "Don't shoot. I'm coming in."

As he approached the fire he saw a wagon drawn up by it. A man and a boy, each with a rifle, stood guarding a picket line of three horses. Two were harness horses and the other had the lines of a saddler.

The wagoner lowered his rifle as Walt came into the firelight. "You're Mason of the JR, ain'tcha?"

"How did you know?"

"We've seen you around Bozeman. I figured to file a homestead on the East Gallatin. But my wife talked me out of it. She's with her folks in Utah and wants me to settle down there. She's a Mormon."

176

Walt explained his chase after two outlaws. "They passed here just as we were turnin' in," the wagoner said. "Seemed kinda funny they didn't make camp; their horses looked played out."

"So's mine." Walt took out his wallet and counted the money in it. The same forty dollars which had made a ceiling for his bid on Lucia's basket was still there. "It's all yours as boot, mister, on a trade for that calico saddle horse."

The boot made it a bargain and the wagoner accepted at once. "Forty dollars'll buy us grub and grain all the way to Utah."

Walt changed saddles. "I grained him right good after sundown," the wagoner said. "He'd orter take you clear to Bozeman."

Midnight found Walt at the top of the Gallatin. He'd passed no other camp, so Ranny was still ahead of him. From here to Bozeman it was only seventy miles, all downgrade.

Walt kneed his mount on. Patches of snow, for a little way, were like ghostly shadows in the moonlight. The trail dipped into a canyon humming with the rushing riffles of the West Gallatin. Always beyond the canyon's next bend he expected to see Ranny's camp.

But there was no camp. The canyon opened into a basin with day dawning as Mason crossed it. Weariness and hunger forced him to stop at Big Spring. "We got to go fifty-five miles yet, Patch." He staked the calico in riverbank grass and ate prodigiously from his grub pack.

At sunrise he rode on, with the fresh sign of four horses still pointing toward Bozeman. Beyond the basin he dropped into another canyon, cliff-bound and narrow. And still no sign of Ranny's camp. "Looks like they aim to go all the way, Patch."

Walt came at last to a familiar landmark, Blackmore's cabin. The latchstring was lout. Walt went in and found a not-quite-empty grain sack. He squeezed out a quart of oats for the calico horse.

"Only thirty miles to Bozeman, Patch. We may beat 'em there yet."

Walt had ridden nearly a third of those thirty miles when he approached the mouth of Spanish Creek. The two outlaws, he estimated, couldn't be more than five miles ahead. So they'd beat him to Bozeman by only an hour. An hour wouldn't be enough, Walt hoped, for Bowers to pack and run.

Two rifle shots clanged on his thought. Two spurts of flame flashed from the Spanish Creek brush. Walt, snatching for his saddle rifle, heard his horse squeal, felt the beast stumble to its knees and go down.

One bullet had gone wild. The other had smashed into the brain of the calico horse. Walt leaped clear of the saddle, landing on his feet with a rifle in hand. He pumped bullets toward the brush from which gunfire had flashed. As he fired the last shot, the calico horse gave a final quiver and died.

Fading hoofbeats came from beyond the brush. Having unhorsed the pursuer, they were making off. It left Walt afoot and helpless. All he could do was trudge on bitterly toward Bozeman.

It was twelve miles downriver to Zeke Sales' sawmill. Twelve miles and four weary hours. Walt Mason limped in and told his story. Men at the mill saddled two fresh horses. One rider went back to salvage Walt's saddle. Walt swung aboard the other horse and spurred angrily toward Bozeman.

Dark was closing in as he reined up at the sheriff's office. McKinzie came out, listened with a grim face, then strode across to the Laclede Hotel.

Two deputies were in the office. One of them brought hot water. Walt took off boots and socks, sat with his feet in the water. "Make a round of the bars, Todd," he told one of the deputies. "Find out if anyone's seen Ike Ranny and a long lean Spaniard named Romero. And, Luke, make a round of the livery barns and look for four horses. Those fellas only got to town three or four hours ago — on played-out mounts."

Todd and Luke hurried out. Then McKinzie came back with a defeated look. "He's gone, Walt. Clerk says a tall, dark cowboy went up to Bowers' room about three hours ago. Bowers came down with a packed grip and checked out. Nobody's seen him since."

Waiting for a report from Todd and Luke gave Walt a chance to tell the complete story of the Idaho raids.

McKinzie bit his lip. "Clint Bowers the cattle buyer! Been sittin' right under our nose for months, smokin' high-priced cigars in the Laclede lobby! And us out beatin' the brush of two counties for him!" Who could doubt, now, that Bowers was the backer mentioned by Dutch Yeager?

Todd and Luke came in. "Nobody's seen Ranny," Todd reported. "But the Spanish guy was seen twice; at the Laclede and at Fridley's barn where he left four played-out horses. Then he bought three fresh horses, paying cash. Rode away on one, leadin' the other two."

McKinzie snapped orders. "Find out which trail they took, Todd. Luke, round up about ten volunteers and get 'em out asking questions. It was broad daylight, so someone's bound to have seen those three ride out of town. Mason; get yourself a room and some sleep."

Walt needed no urging. He took supper at the Laclede and went to bed. He slept eight hours and was at an early breakfast when McKinzie joined him. "We know which way they went, Walt."

"Yeh?"

"They were seen riding up Bridger Creek about dark. Like they were heading for Bridger Pass. If they rode all night they'll be on Shields River by now. Todd and Luke are saddling up to take off after them."

"Saddle up for me too." Walt left the table. At a lobby rack he picked up his hat and gunbelt.

The sheriff caught up with him. "You're in no shape for it, Walt."

The JR foreman was stubborn. "I was right there when Ranny killed Chuck Ward in cold blood. Then he shot a good horse out from under me. I'm off after him, Sheriff."

Presently he was loping east with Todd and Luke. "You sure they went up Bridger Creek, Luke?"

"Dead sure. The miller at Story's flour mill saw 'em pass. He knows Bowers by sight. About two hours after

180

that Fritz Schwind saw 'em cross his ditch, up Bridger Creek. They were riding in the woods, a piece off the trail, like they wanted to keep outa sight."

At the flour mill the miller confirmed his testimony. Farther on Fritz Schwind did the same. "You can see their tracks," Schwind said, "where they crossed my ditch."

He led them to the spot. Hoof marks of three horses, heading up-canyon, were plain in the ditchbank mud. Walt took a close look. "One horse," he said, "has a flat shoe on the left forehoof. A narrow shoe with the calks missing."

The very fact that the three men had kept to the woods was enough to identify them. Walt and the deputies followed the tracks and after a mile or so they veered back into the trail. "They tried to keep out of sight till dark," Luke reasoned. "Dark caught them about here so they took to the main trail."

Halfway to the pass a homesteader was building a cabin by the road. His family was housed in a tent there. Todd checked with him. "Did you see three men ride uptrail last night, about two hours after dark?"

"No, but I heard 'em. I'd gone to bed. Sounded like they were off the trail a piece, over by that gravel bank."

Walt looked at ground near the gravel bank. "Here's that same shoe print," he reported. "Ridin' by here they got off the trail a little so the tent family wouldn't see 'em."

Once on Bridger Pass, and twice on Brackett Creek beyond it, they found the print of a calkless front-left horseshoe. Walt and the deputies stayed all night at a

Brackett Creek ranch. The ranch people hadn't seen the fugitives pass.

In the morning Walt found the sign of flight once more. At the mouth of Brackett Creek the fugitives had ridden into the Shields River riffles. A sandy bank showed the marks plainly.

But they didn't emerge on the river's other side.

Luke rode upriver and Todd rode down. Walt called at five Shields River ranches hoping that Bowers and his guides had been seen. It was all for nothing. The sign had disappeared completely in the Shields River riffles.

After another baffled day Walt and the deputies rode down Shields River to its junction with the Yellowstone. They inquired at Benson's Landing. Both the storeman and the stage station people knew Bowers well. "But we haven't seen him lately, Walt."

They wasted still another day inquiring along the Yellowstone. Then, jaded and discouraged, Walt and the deputies started home by the stage road which ran over Bozeman Pass.

They spent a night at Hopper's change station and by noon the next day were riding down the west slope toward Ten Mile. No stage was due, so the Ten Mile dining room wasn't open. "Maybe we can get some coffee," Walt said as he dismounted at the hitchrail.

They went in and the station master's wife brought them coffee. A thin, wiry man with bowed legs and a holstered gun stood at the bar with whisky. At first Walt paid him no attention. Then, as he raised a cup to his lips, the JR foreman suddenly spilled coffee on his shirt.

He leaned across the table to whisper: "Don't look now, boys. But as we pass out take a quick squint at him. The little guy at the bar."

Walt paid the bill and led the way out. At the hitchrail he asked, "Did you see him?"

"Sure," Luke said. "He's Monk Tucker. Used to rack balls at a Bozeman pool hall. Got in trouble about a year ago and I haven't seen him since."

"Follow me." Walt mounted and rode on down the stage road toward Bozeman. But at the first screen of brush he stopped. "Let's take cover, and watch. I want to see where that fella goes."

"You mean Monk Tucker? Why?"

"The gun he's wearing has a wooden grip. Black wood with a crack in it. I've seen that gun before. It belongs to a friend of mine named Rolfe Kendall."

CHAPTER
SIXTEEN

Presently they saw Tucker leave the station and mount a pony. The man rode uptrail toward the Pass. Walt watched him splash across Jackson Creek and go a little way beyond it. Then the man stopped and looked both ways along the stage road. When it appeared as if no one was in sight, he left the trail and rode easterly toward a wooded gap in the hills.

A small creek came out of that gap and Tucker disappeared into its brushy ravine.

"Let's go, boys." Todd and Luke kept pace as Walt rode at a brisk gait to follow the man. When they came to the ravine they found a flow of water only a step wide and an inch or two deep. "What's at the head of it?" Walt asked.

"They call it Timberline Creek," Luke said. "There's coal land at the top of it. Nobody lives there."

"Your man Tucker does," Walt argued. "And he's got Kendall's gun."

A dim trail led up the creeklet's left bank. It was meant only for saddle horses, yet Walt made out faint tire tracks of a wagon. "A wonder it didn't tip over, on this hillside."

The pine timber thickened and a short way into it the trail was barred by a wire fence. A plank gate in the fence had a padlock on it; and a sign which said:

PRIVATE PROPERTY
KEEP OUT
TIMBERLINE COAL COMPANY

Deputy Todd squinted thoughtfully at the name. "It's an honest outfit, Walt. Strictly on the level. Now I remember."

"Remember what?"

"Last year when somebody found a big coal seam up this way, a corporation bought up a couple of thousand acres. They had a crew up here to drive a test tunnel and sink a few test pits. The papers said their engineers reported enough coal up here to mine a hundred thousand tons a year for ten years."

"Then why didn't they go after it?"

"There won't be any market for coal till the railroad gets here, which won't be for a couple of years yet. So the company fenced the place, padlocked the gate and moved out. They'll come back just as soon as N.P. trains start comin' over Bozeman Pass."

"Did they leave a caretaker?"

Todd shook his head. "Why should they? Nothin' to take care of except a few empty shacks where the test crew lived."

Walt took pliers from his saddle bag and cut the fence. They rode silently through and on. The trail led them through a narrow cut with the piny slopes on either side getting steeper.

"The *Courier* had an article about it," Todd remembered, "when the crew was testing here. It said the plan was to run a narrow-gauge spur from the main line, soon as it gets over the pass."

Abruptly the ravine opened into a marsh of small beaver dams. On the south side of it was a gently sloping park of lodgepole pines, while the steeper north slope was bare. Black tailing heaps marked a tunnel and three test pits, all on the north side. The floor of the little valley was a mesh of willow brush along a chain of shallow beaver ponds. Fronting these ponds were four rude log shacks. One had been a blacksmith shop for the sharpening of test tools. All four seemed to be deserted.

"Maybe Tucker kept right on going," Luke suggested.

"And maybe he didn't," Walt brooded. "For an outlaw hide-out you couldn't beat this place. Nobody'd suspect a big coal corporation. Tucker could hole up here snug as a bug in a rug for the next two years."

They tied their mounts and moved forward afoot. Each carried a rifle in his left hand and a short gun in his right. As the trees thinned Walt spotted a fifth shack, until now hidden by the willows. "Looks like a horse shed; that's why we don't see Tucker's horse."

The four log shacks all had flat sod roofs. One was windowless and could have been used as a powder house. Back of the nearest one lay a pile of unrusted tin cans. "Cover me," Walt said, "while I slip up to a window."

"I'll tag along myself," Todd insisted. He was the senior deputy. "Cover us, Luke."

Luke crouched back of a windfall with his rifle. Walt Mason, with Todd siding him, advanced quietly toward the nearest shack. They were less than halfway to it when its door opened. Nothing came out except a panful of water. Then the door was pushed shut.

Walt and Todd paused for a minute, eyes and ears open. A small trout jumped in one of the ponds. Otherwise a complete silence ruled the valley.

"Tucker's in there," Walt whispered.

"Him and who else?" Todd wondered.

"Let's find out."

They moved on toward the shack which on this side had no window. Twenty paces short of it they came onto soft ground. Overflow from a beaver dam had made streaks of mud. Todd's boot made a squishing sound and brought a voice from the cabin. "What was that, Tuck?"

"One of them damn mudhens, Jody. The ponds are lousy with 'em."

Walt and Todd exchanged glances. At least two men were in there. "This is it!" Walt murmured. He quickened his advance with Todd keeping at his elbow.

The shot came from high on a steep bare hillside to their right. Walt looked up there and saw a rifleman aiming for a second shot.

But the second shot came from Luke, crouching behind a windfall to cover the advance. As it rang out two men burst from the shack, each with a cocked gun. Each began shooting on sight and Walt, returning the fire, at the same time heard a rap-rap of rifle shots being exchanged between Luke and the man upslope.

Todd hit the mud with a bleeding shoulder but fired once more from his knees. Walt Mason was unhit and knew why. A shiny badge on Todd's vest had drawn the fire of both Jody and Tucker. As Todd fell, Walt dropped Jody. His next shot missed Tucker. Then Tucker looked upslope and dropped his gun. What he saw up there brought his quick surrender.

Walt himself looked up the hill and saw the rifleman rolling down it. He was a burly, barrel-chested man. A shot from Luke had either killed or winged him.

Luke came running from his windfall. He stooped beside Todd and found he had only a flesh wound. Walt hurried forward to pick up Tucker's gun. Jody had been hit in the breast and was dead. Upslope, the rolling rifleman came to a stop against the black tailings of a test pit. Higher up, at the spot where he'd opened fire, Walt saw a fresh-cut quarter of venison. Evidently the man had been returning from a meat hunt.

This shack was empty. Walt moved on to the next; then to the next. The last one had no windows and a padlocked door. Walt rattled the lock and shouted, "Are you in there, Rolfe?"

There was no response. Then Luke came up with a key he'd found in Tucker's pockets. "See if it fits, Walt."

It did. On the shack's dark damp floor Rolfe Kendall lay in a stupor. He was bruised, feverish, half-starved. Out in the sunlight he opened his eyes and saw Walt

Mason. A pale smile came to his sunken, bearded face. "Thanks," he murmured faintly.

"Let's get him to Ten Mile and a square meal," Walt said.

Doctor Monroe went up to Ten Mile station on the morning stage. After bandaging Todd's shoulder, he spent the rest of the day there treating Rolfe Kendall, then took Rolfe down to Bozeman on the evening stage. "All you need is good food and a soft bed, young fellow. Take a room at the hotel and stay in it till I say when."

By that time the coroner had gathered up two dead men, Hunker and Jody, and Luke had lodged Tucker in the county jail.

Rolfe was sitting up in bed with a supper tray in his lap when Walt came in with McKinzie. "If you feel up to it," the sheriff said, "let's go over it again."

Kendall gave it to them again. How he'd looked on at the Delmonico while Jody won big money with dice. His suspicion that it was a pay-off for the sniping of Kim Dallas. "By the way, how is that boy, Walt?"

Mason grinned. "He's kinda like you, too tough to kill. I promised him a job at the JR, soon as he can fork a saddle. Go on."

Rolfe touched the highlights of his prowl in a Third Street cabin. "They socked me and hauled me to that Timberline hide-out."

"Which explains," Walt said, "why we couldn't find a patched-eye halfbreed at the other hideaway, down in Idaho. The guy was Jody made up that way."

"You must have heard them talking," McKinzie broke in impatiently. "I mean Jody and Hunker and Tuck. What did they say?"

"They mentioned a man named Clint. Hunker said I was being kept alive to trade with, in case Clint got in a tight spot. Soon as everything was safe, I was to be gunned and dropped into a test pit."

"In that case," Walt grimaced, "we showed up just in time. Clint's out of his tight spot now; he got clean away."

"What else," the sheriff prompted, "did they say about Clint?"

Rolfe forked a morsel of steak to his mouth and chewed it thoughtfully. "Far as I can remember, they only mentioned Clint one other time. First few days Tuck was there alone with me. Then Hunker and Jody came up from town and brought a bottle. They were passing it around outside my door and I heard some talk."

"About what?"

"About soldiers' scrip. Tuck asked if Clint had any more of that soldiers' scrip. Hunker didn't know; but he was sure Clint had used scrip to pick up a land title down in Idaho."

"What else?"

"That's all. I never heard 'em mention Clint again."

McKinzie mulled it over. "We can't hang him for using scrip to get a land title," he decided. "Lots of honest ranches have been put together that way. Stockmen of high standing, like Granville Stuart to name just one, have used soldiers' scrip to pick up land titles. The scrip's assignable, just like government bonds."

"Let's hear your end of it, Walt?" Rolfe begged.

Mason told about the foray into Idaho. "One man killed on our side and two on theirs. Wilder took a bullet in the leg. We picked up two prisoners, Monte Brucker and a man named Nash. And one stolen steer."

"Is the posse back?"

"Not yet. They had to attend a coroner's inquest down there, over the bodies of Chuck Ward, Dakota and Tex Orme."

Rolfe looked at McKinzie. "Are you going to arrest Mr. Fancy Vest at the Delmonico? The guy they call Chips Charny?"

The sheriff gave a disgruntled negative. "What could I charge him with? It's just a guess about those eight straight passes Jody made. It was all out in the open, with fifty people looking on."

"We've got the goods on Clint Bowers," Walt agreed, "but we've nothing that ties him to Charny."

McKinzie picked up his hat. "That's our number-one job, boys: to dig up a link between Charny and Bowers."

CHAPTER
SEVENTEEN

The link was elusive. Regular customers at the Delmonico were questioned, many of them men of good standing, and not one of them had ever seen Bowers at Charny's bar.

Charny himself admitted knowing Bowers by sight. "But he never spent a dime in my place, Sheriff." Rhonda the hostess, as well as the bar and game crews, backed him up.

Two prisoners in the county jail, Yeager and Tucker, were grilled patiently. "Yeager, you're waiting trial for murder. It won't hurt you to cooperate a little. Just how is your backer, Clint Bowers, tied up with Chips Charny?"

"Far as I know, they've had no truck with each other," Yeager said, and stuck to it.

McKinzie turned to the other prisoner. "Tuck, your friend Jody died with twelve hundred dollars on him. Was it a pay-off for sniping young Dallas?"

"Nuts! He won it fair and square, in a crap game."

A posse returned from Idaho with two new prisoners, Brucker and Nash. They were booked for steer-stealing. "Did Chips Charny ever show up at that Idaho hideaway?"

"Of course not," Brucker said. "What would a Fancy Dan like Charny be doin' away out there in the woods?"

"I was only the cook," Nash kept saying.

Walt Mason, after a few days at the ranch, came back to town and made a try himself. Rolfe Kendall was on his feet by then. Walt took him to the Delmonico, at the peak of evening trade, to look the place over.

It was the usual scene: the platinum-blond Rhonda floating about in a Paris gown, charming customers, flirting with the best prospects, coaxing them into games; De Shon the spotter, perched on a stool, gunslung and steel-eyed as he looked the crowd over for trouble. And Charny himself, short, wide and as flashy as ever, presiding over it all. He spoke suavely to Walt and Rolfe, then moved off to spell his house man at the dice board.

"Just like when Jody cleaned up," Rolfe whispered.

Again this time the customer won, although for small stakes. Was it a play to the gallery? Walt wondered.

Rhonda came up to bewitch them. "Are you having a good time, gentlemen? What may I bring you?"

"Not a thing, Mrs. Charny," Walt said.

Rhonda took no offense. As she moved away Rolfe asked, "You mean she's Charny's wife?"

"Sure she is. They live in the old Hartcorn house, right across the alley; eat three meals a day there and send out the family wash, just like any other married couple. The transient customers don't know it, though: cowboys and freighters and boomers. Rhonda lets them think she's single and wide open for romance; that way she can make them spend more money."

A mild little man with a carnation in his buttonhole came in. He was Ridley Davis, of Davis and Davis. "Take a message out to Barry Rodman for me, Walt," the lawyer said.

"Okay, Mr. Davis. What is it?"

"Anceney, Fratt and the MacAndows have retained us to file litigation against Clinton Bowers. As executors of the John Rodman estate, we're joining them in the same action. It's to recover fourteen thousand dollars paid to Bowers in Omaha for twelve cars of stolen steers, plus costs."

"Good!" Walt said. "Can you put it over?"

"We'll put it over in two moves," the lawyer explained. "First we'll get a judgment against Bowers for fifteen thousand. Next, to satisfy that judgment we'll attach the assets of the Targhee Cattle Co., alias Lou Harrison, alias Clinton Bowers. Said assets will include any cash we find on Bowers when we catch him. Whatever we recover will go to pay the four ranches in proportion to the number of steers each lost."

"I'll tell Barry," Walt promised.

"By the way, here's some mail for him." Ridley Davis handed Walt a letter, finished his drink and went out.

Perry Hamil, in his room at the ranch the next afternoon, read the letter carefully. Three others from the girl in Roanoke had awaited him on his return from Idaho. From first to last he'd received eight and when

194

considered in sequence they told the story of a troubled mind; a disturbed mind and a hurt heart which for a while had tried to make light of its own fears.

Hamil destroyed this one, as he'd destroyed them all. But another sequence he'd kept — the various issues of the Bozeman *Courier* which had come out since his arrival here. He took them in hand now to reread certain items of news and gossip; a total of five items linking Lucia Ripley's name with Barry Rodman's.

The Virginia girl was sure to have read them. Except for one hard fact they would have meant little to her. But the hard fact was there. Her fiancé, Barry Rodman, hadn't written her a single line since meeting that girl on the stage!

The intervals between her letters were getting longer; a tone of restraint was growing more and more evident. At first she'd inquired gayly about the "beautiful damsel" he'd carried from the river. But in this last letter she made no mention of Lucia. She wrote mainly, and rather dully, about her own life in Roanoke. And in this one she didn't mention her failure to get responses from Bozeman. Only a hard-hit pride, on guard to hide despair, would make her do that. She ended the letter, "Hoping to hear from you soon, as ever, Diane."

In it Hamil could feel her chilling fear. She was beginning to know she'd lost him. Yet it was equally clear that she had no faint suspicion of his masquerade. As he burned the letter, Perry Hamil wondered if he'd ever hear from her again.

The roundup was over and tonight the Chinese cook served the JR's full crew at supper. Mason, Hamil,

Kendall, Pony Willard and a middle-aged rider named Mack Boyd. Boyd had repped the outfit at the roundup during its last week.

"We'll need two extra hands in August," Walt explained to Hamil, "when we put up hay. Then we'll be ready for the beef drive in October."

"What beef drive?" Hamil used every chance to show his ignorance of ranching operations. Every minute he must play the part of Barry Rodman.

"Our hay crop," Walt told him, "will only be enough to winter cows with calves and cows due to have calves in the spring. Means we'd better ship all he-stuff over two years old, and all dry cows, to market."

"What market?"

"Chicago. The papers say that the rails will be laid as far as Glendive by November. So we'll drive the stuff to Glendive, on the Dakota-Montana line, car it there and ship it to Chicago by way of St. Paul."

"How long will it take, this cattle drive to Glendive?"

"It's three hundred and sixty miles. At thirteen miles a day it'll take about four weeks. Want to go along, boss?"

"No thanks." Hamil had no stomach for riding back through Miles City where the real Barry Rodman lay buried. Except for an occasional date with Lucia Ripley, he'd made up his mind to stick right here on the ranch well out of sight of people like Harry De Shon.

"You can send me, if it's okay," Rolfe Kendall offered. "I always did want to see Chicago."

There was a week of irrigating and of catching up with routine work which had been slighted because of the Idaho excursion. Hamil helped out, laboring like a common hand. After hours he practiced with his six-gun at the shed wall target, making just the right scores to be plausible.

Walt and Rolfe talked much about the hue and cry after Bowers. "I'd sure like to nail that guy; him and the Ike Ranny," Walt kept saying. "I was caught flat-footed at that tavern, when Ranny gunned Chuck Ward."

Rolfe nodded restlessly. "I wonder if the sheriff ever dug up a link between Charny and Bowers."

On the second week end they rode in to find out. Hamil went along with them, mainly in the hope of seeing Lucia.

He found her in Doctor Monroe's place over the drugstore. She'd brought a box of sweets to cheer up Kim Dallas.

"Thanks, Miss Lucia. But stop treatin' me like a baby," the boy protested. His cheeks were showing color and he was sitting up in bed. "Mr. Rodman, when do I get that job at the ranch?"

"Just the minute you're able to ride out there," Hamil promised. "And I wrote your folks back East, Kim. Told 'em you're doing fine; told 'em we'll have a good river-bottom half-section picked out for 'em when they trail out here in the spring; told 'em there's an empty cabin on the JR they can use while they're building one of their own."

That last was news to Lucia. She held out both hands impulsively. "That's just like you, Barry. You're just about the sweetest, kindest man I ever knew."

"In that case, what about a Sunday date? I can show up with the smartest rig in town and we'll take a drive up Bear Canyon."

"Tomorrow? Oh, but I can't. Walt's coming out. Didn't he tell you?"

Hamil made a face. "Serves me right. I should have asked you sooner. What about a week from Sunday?"

"I'll be expecting you, Barry."

Hamil went looking for Walt and Rolfe and found them at McKinzie's office. They were huddled over a wire which had just come in from Billings. "It's about that Spaniard, Romero," the sheriff announced. "They've picked him up."

"Where?"

"He rode into a horse trader's corral at Billings, leading two horses. Tried to sell them. But the trader checked with the Billings sheriff. I'd sent a description of those mounts to every county in Montana. They were the ones Bowers and Ranny escaped on — bought at Fridley's barn here in Bozeman. So they've got Romero in jail in Billings. I'm sending Jack Todd to bring him back on the stage."

"What about Bowers and Ranny?"

"Romero says he left them in a deserted ranch house on Clark's Fork. Deputies went to that ranch and found no one there."

"Sounds fishy," Walt muttered. "If Bowers and Ranny wanted to hide at a ranch, why would they let Romero take away all three mounts?"

"Maybe they didn't!" Rolfe Kendall had a gleam in his eye. "Look, Walt. You said you and Todd and Luke followed tracks of three horses over Bridger Pass and lost 'em in the Shields River riffles?"

"That's right. So we know that the three of them were together at least that far."

"No you don't," Rolfe argued. "You know three *horses* were together — but suppose two of the horses had empty saddles!"

Walt and the sheriff gaped at him. "Come again, Rolfe."

"The three men," Kendall reminded them, "were last seen together by Fritz Schwind only seven miles from Bozeman. It was at nightfall. Suppose Bowers and Ranny dismounted right there and doubled back afoot to hide in Bozeman; while Romero fooled you by leading two empty-saddle horses on over the pass!"

"It doesn't make sense!" Walt protested.

McKinzie didn't think so either. He had a man watching the old Third Street cabin once used by Jody and Hunker on a chance that others of the gang might show up there.

"Did you ever search Chips Charny's safe?" Rolfe asked him.

"Search it for what?"

"Soldiers' scrip, for one thing." Rolfe looked across Main Street and saw a merchant in the doorway of his store. He stepped out on the sidewalk and shouted,

"Mr. Cram, would you mind coming over here a minute?"

When Adam Cram joined them, Rolfe asked a single question. "On the stage from Miles City in June, Mr. Cram, Chips Charny's name came up. You said he once ran a trading store on the Oregon Trail and lost his license for three reasons: suspicion of selling liquor to Indians, suspicion of trading rifles to Indians, and — what was the third reason?"

"They claim he took advantage of stranded immigrants. Some of 'em had land scrip and he made 'em sign it over to 'em for bacon and flour. Charged 'em forty prices. They say he picked up a whole hatful of that scrip before the government canceled his license."

"Thanks. That's all, Mr. Cram."

Adam Cram left them and Rolfe said: "Remember that talk I heard between Tuck and Hunker. About Clint Bowers using scrip to get an Idaho land title. Where did Bowers get that scrip? Maybe from Chips Charny. If Charny put up the scrip, he's a silent partner in the Targhee Cattle Company."

"In which case," Walt added, "there might be something in Charny's safe to prove it."

McKinzie chewed on it a minute, then left, the room. He came back with a search warrant. It authorized a search of the Delmonico for loaded dice or daubed cards.

"It's routine." The sheriff grinned. "We do it every three or four months. Whenever a man files a complaint claiming he's been cold-decked at some joint, we look the place over. Chips Charny expects it and so we never find anything. He's too smart."

McKinzie sent for Wilder and set up a routine raid. "This time we'll make him open the safe, to look for trick decks and dice. But what we'll really look for is paper. Anything to show a deal between Charny and Bowers. Want to come along, Walt?"

"Sure I do," Walt said.

"Me too," Rolfe echoed.

It made a raiding party of four and when they went out Perry Hamil was left alone in the office. He would have offered to go himself except for Harry De Shon. That loose-triggered ex-marshal would be on guard at the bar.

Not that De Shon would resist the raid. In his peace-officer days he himself must have made many similar raids. He'd get a reassuring nod from Charny, likely, then merely stand by to look cynically on. Yet Hamil couldn't bring himself to run the gantlet of the man's critical inspection. It might bring back an elusive memory of a night, five years ago, in a Kansas jail.

So Hamil sat alone, waiting. Minutes slipped by and he heard no shooting. Therefore the raid wasn't being resisted. By now the raiders would be searching the safe.

Whatever they found there could hardly concern Perry Hamil. It would make a news story for the *Courier* and a topic for bar talk all around town. Which in turn would make just one more diversion here in Bozeman, giving people just that much less time to size up a young heir from Virginia who called himself Barry Rodman.

Till now he'd courted publicity. It had served his purpose — to impress a reader in Roanoke — but he wanted no more of it. From here on he should stay out of the limelight, letting time flow smoothly by till the settlement of an estate.

Sooner than he expected the raiders came back. McKinzie, Mason and Wilder had defeated looks; clearly they'd found nothing of importance. But Kendall came in grinning. The grin was almost smug as he perched on a desk near Hamil.

"Find any of that scrip?" Hamil asked.

"Not a scrap of it."

"Any partnership papers?"

"Not one blame thing," Wilder reported glumly, "to show a tie-up between Charny and Bowers."

"Nothing but a marriage paper," Rolfe amended. "A woman generally takes good care of her marriage certificate. That blond hostess keeps hers in the Delmonico safe."

"So what?" McKinzie said. "It's no secret. We've always known they were man and wife; Rhonda and Chips Charny."

"You should've read clear through that certificate," Rolfe chided, "like I did. It gives the gal's maiden name; the one she had before she married Charny."

The others stared. "Yeh? Who was she?"

"She was born Rhonda Bowers," Rolfe told them. "There's the tie we've been lookin' for. A blood tie. Brothers-in-law, Charny and Bowers are. What about setting up another raid, Sheriff? That house across the alley from the Delmonico's back door, where the Charnys live. It's got a spare bedroom, likely. A room big enough for Rhonda's hide-away brother; and maybe for his bodyguard, Ike Ranny."

CHAPTER
EIGHTEEN

In the cool twilight of that Saturday evening McKinzie quietly deployed his forces. Wilder and Mason covered the front, with Rolfe Kendall and Deputy Luke Scott in the alley. The house, a nine-room frame facing Mendenhall Street, had tall shuttered windows and wide porches both front and back. Several small balconies jutted out from the second floor. All through the seventies it had been the home of the Hartcorns, a highly respectable pioneer family. Lately the Charnys had leased it because of its convenience to the Delmonico.

This evening Sheriff McKinzie entered the Delmonico from Main Street, search warrant in hand.

Trade was brisk, all bar space taken. Charny smiled tolerantly as McKinzie approached him. "Did you forget something, Sheriff?" he quipped.

Rhonda glided up and took the sheriff's arm. "Of course he did, Chips. He forgot to buy me a drink."

McKinzie shook her off and thrust a paper into Charny's hand. "Read it; it's for you too, Mrs. Charny."

The paper authorized a search of a certain house, on suspicion that outlaws were hiding there. One look and all the swagger went out of Charny. His ruddiness faded and his voice took a pitch of despair. "You can't do it; it's my private home; I'll sue you; you've no right . . ."

"The warrant says I have. The house is surrounded right now."

Fifty people at bar and games heard it. The room was suddenly tense and still, all eyes staring this way.

By now Rhonda had read the warrant. She tried to make light of it. "Don't be silly, Sheriff. The only outlaws we know are already in your jail."

"What about your brother Clint?" As McKinzie spoke the name the woman wilted. Her shoulders drooped. A gray fear stripped her of glamour and made her look tired and old. "And his bodyguard Ranny," the sheriff added.

Charny turned desperately toward De Shon. "Stop them, Harry," he pleaded. "Don't let them . . ."

De Shon broke in stolidly. "I'm hired to keep order at this bar; not to fight a crew of peace officers serving a legal warrant on a private house. I used to be a peace officer myself."

McKinzie held out his hand. "What about giving me a key, Charny? It'll save crashing a door." When the saloonman failed to give him a key, the sheriff shrugged and offered a warning. "You and Rhonda better not try a runout. You wouldn't get far."

He left them and went out by the alley exit.

In the alley Kendall reported, "The doors are all locked, Sheriff."

"Shall I bat out a window?" Luke offered.

"Go ahead, Luke."

Luke pried a shutter loose and broke the glass of a lower window. No one challenged as he climbed inside. A minute later he unbolted a kitchen door to admit McKinzie.

"Stay in the alley, Rolfe," the sheriff ordered. "Watch those upper balconies in case someone jumps out that way."

They let Walt Mason in at the front. Deputy Wilder stayed in the street. The sheriff called to him, "Bowers could be in an upstairs room; when he hears us he may try to jump out."

"If he does I'll nail him," Wilder promised.

"And don't overlook Ranny," Walt warned.

"It'll be a pleasure." Wilder limped to mid-street and took a stand there with his rifle. He was in a position to sweep the upper balconies on either side of the house; and so was Rolfe at the rear.

It was almost dark and the street was filling up. A crowd from the Main Street bars had rounded the block and stood watching, whispering, waiting. None of them knew the steps of reasoning which had led up to this raid: the possibility that two of three fugitives had turned back from Bridger Canyon; soldiers' scrip possibly passed from Charny to Bowers; and the marriage certificate of Rhonda Bowers Charny. But at least fifty of them had seen the stark panic on Charny's face just now. Unless he was hiding something in this house, why would Charny be afraid?

So the crowd watched in morbid silence as dark fell over Mendenhall Street. They saw glows appear at lower floor windows as the sheriff's men lighted lamps in there. They saw Wilder in mid-street and Rolfe in the alley, each with a ready rifle.

Inside, McKinzie, Luke and Walt searched the ground floor room by room. Then Luke, with a lamp in his left hand and a cocked gun in his right, went down steep steps into a cellar. His voice called up to them, "Nobody down here, Sheriff."

"Let's take a look upstairs," McKinzie said.

Before he could start up Walt Mason brushed by and got ahead of him. "Chuck Ward was a buddy of mine, Sheriff. I owe him something for the way I bungled that play at the tavern."

They moved single file up the narrow stairs, first Mason, then McKinzie, then Luke Scott. Walt and Luke each carried a lamp. At the top of the stairs Walt put his lamp on a hall table. The hall had five inner doors. Every transom was dark. McKinzie took a stand by Walt and shouted, "We're too many for you, Bowers; might as well come out."

No answer. Walt wondered if they could be wrong. Maybe the Charnys were hiding something other than outlaws here; maybe incriminating papers or stolen money. It would account for their panic at the bar.

They began at the rearmost of five hall doors and worked toward the front. The fact that it wasn't locked meant no one was hiding there. While Luke and the sheriff covered it with guns, Walt pushed it open. Luke's lamp showed a neatly made bedroom, quite empty. It was the same when they opened the second door.

Then Walt, twisting the third knob, found the door locked. He held his gun to the lock and shot it off. McKinzie yelled: "This is your last call, Bowers. Come on out."

Still no answer. Walt kicked the door open and stepped quickly to one side. A roar came from the room's darkness and a bullet zinged through the doorway. "Come and get me!" The voice wasn't Bowers' but Ike Ranny's.

"Okay," Walt said. "Just like you got Chuck Ward." He nodded to Luke and it was a prearranged signal. Luke tossed his lighted lamp through the doorway. It landed with a crash on the floor. Walt was peering warily in and the momentary flash showed him Ranny. The man was crouched in a corner with a leveled gun.

Walt, exposing only one arm and half his face, fired five fast shots toward that corner. The flashes showed Ranny shooting back. The man's first bullet breathed on Walt but the next one went wild. Walt heard a bump on the floor; after that the room was dark and silent.

It was a quiet broken by shouts from the street. A rifle cracked from the alley. With a dull thud something hit the ground under a balcony; it was an upper balcony jutting from the next room up the hall.

"I think you got him, Walt," Luke said. "And somebody else got Bowers."

For a minute more they waited for a sound from Ranny. Then Luke brought another lamp and they saw him in the room's far corner. He lay doubled up there; the gun had fallen free from his hand.

208

Luke shot the lock off the next door and found a slept-in bed, an open balcony window, and no occupant. He stepped out on the balcony and looked down at Clinton Bowers. Rolfe Kendall shouted up: "I missed him, Luke. But the drop broke his arm. What next?"

An answer came gruffly from McKinzie. "Lock him up. Then send the coroner over here to pick up Ranny. And Wilder, get out warrants for the Charnys. We're jailing them both."

"On what charge, Sheriff?"

"Harboring outlaws, suspicion of stealing cattle, and suspicion of hiring Jody to snipe Kim Dallas."

It was a night of shock for Bozeman. In all its raw history, since the pathfinder John Bozeman had first set foot here seventeen years earlier, there'd never been a Saturday night like this one. Every bar was full and no one slept. Lobbies and sidewalks seethed with speculations.

And again Perry Hamil looked on it as grist for his own mill of deception. The spotlight was on Bowers and the Charnys. Would they be convicted on all three counts? The case against the Charnys seemed solid only on the first count, harboring outlaws.

Hamil got away from it early in the morning. He rode back to the ranch with his mind made up to stay there. Every passing week would establish him more securely in the shoes of Barry Rodman, bringing closer each day the John Rodman fortune.

A day later Walt and Rolfe came out with a new issue of the *Courier*. The headlines were jubilant. The entire ring, the paper said, had now been wiped out or jailed. Steers would no longer mysteriously disappear from the Gallatin County ranges. Nothing remained but to bury the dead and convict the eight surviving crooks: Bowers, Yeager, Nash, Brucker, Tucker, Romero and the Charnys. "It's all over but the shouting!" the *Courier* said.

Reading it, Hamil could only hope they'd keep on thinking like that. He himself knew it *wasn't* all over. There was still his own masquerade as Barry Rodman. And there was still the stalking menace of Harry De Shon. They'd closed up the Delmonico and so De Shon was out of a job. Would he stay in Bozeman, or move on?

July slipped by and except for one Sunday-afternoon date with Lucia Ripley, Hamil stayed clear of town.

Then August came and brought haying time. Hamil pitched in with the others, driving a sulky rake, then forking shocks to the hay wagon which Pony Willard drove to the stack pen.

Not since the raid on the Charnys had there been any letter from Virginia. The girl had taken the hint, Hamil concluded. Pride wouldn't let her write any more.

By the end of August the last stack of cured vega was topped off and weighted against fall winds. A minstrel show was on at the Bozeman theatre and Walt Mason had a date to take Lucia there. As the foreman rode away Pony Willard glanced slyly toward Hamil. "Looks like he's one up on you, Barry."

The entire county had become aware of a rivalry between master and foreman at the JR. It didn't worry Hamil. The blue chips were all on his own side of the table. Walt was only a fifty-dollar cowboy, in no position to marry a girl like Lucia. She'd been brought up in the sheltered life of army posts and she'd hardly exchange it for what Mason could offer.

That week end he stayed quietly on the ranch, except to plunk away a few times at his shed-wall target.

Early Monday Walt came back from town. "Some mail for you, Barry." He handed Hamil a small square package.

Hamil knew at once that it was from the girl in Virginia. He took it to his room, broke the wax seal and looked inside. There was no message. Just a ring with a solitaire diamond in it!

By train and river boat and stage it had come the long weary way from Virginia. An engagement ring returned from a broken heart — to Barry Rodman of Bozeman, Montana.

CHAPTER
NINETEEN

For Hamil it cleared away the last real hazard. He was rid of her at last and could breathe easier now. She was a link to Barry Rodman's past. As long as it hung over him there'd always been a danger that she'd wire to someone else out here, possibly the lawyers, and ask questions. Any inquiry at all would have scuttled Hamil. The fact that she'd made none proved that she'd never had the slightest shadow of suspicion.

Now the curtain was dropped, once and for all. Her bruised pride would do the rest, and she'd never mention him again.

The crisp days of September came and during the first three weeks of it Hamil only ventured twice to town. On alternate Sundays he rented Fridley's best rig and drove out to Fort Ellis for a date with Lucia Ripley. Fridley grinned as he handed the reins to Hamil. "Makes you even-steven with Walt. He had this same outfit last week."

Many in Bozeman wore that same grin, on Sunday afternoons, as they watched first Hamil and then his foreman drive out to the post. The sentry at the stockade gate was no exception, as he passed the rivals in and out. The *Courier's* "Local Briefs" column handled it obliquely: "Mr. Nip of the JR passed through town Sunday; we wish him luck, and the same goes for his foreman, Mr. Tuck."

Sackett's bartender had another name for it. "Nip-and-Tuck my eye! What chance has Walt Mason got, against a gent like Barry Rodman?"

"You can't always tell about females," a customer disputed. "They don't always pick the guy with the biggest bankroll."

"I'll lay three to one this one will," the barman offered.

At the ranch, gathering beef was the main activity during late September. Everything with the John Rodman brand on it was brought close in and divided into two bunches. Cows with calves-by-side, and cows due for early calves, were to be kept and winter-fed; while all other cows and he-stuff above yearling age must go to market.

It would make a shipment of about three hundred head and Rolfe Kendall, with Mack Boyd assigned to help him, got the driving job. "Start pushin' 'em east on October first," Walt directed. "If you start later'n that you might run into snowstorms."

"It'll put me in Chicago," Rolfe calculated, "around the sixth of November."

All summer the Northern Pacific had been laying track across Dakota at the rate of a mile per day. Shipments were to be accepted at Glendive, on the Montana side of the line, by the end of October. "Soon as you get the stuff carred, Rolfe, send Boyd back home and you can ride the caboose to Chicago."

Beef shipments were the life blood of Montana and so this one made a news item for the *Courier*. Editor Alderson called at the ranch to get facts and figures. Mason gave them to him. "We're billing it to the Clay-Robinson Commission Company. Rolfe Kendall'll go all the way with it."

Alderson made a note, then glanced curiously toward a shed wall riddled with bullet holes.

Walt smiled. "That's where Barry's been practicin'. He was a bum shot right at first. But he never gave up. Now he makes a bull's-eye every time."

The newsman chuckled. "Shows you what perseverance'll do." Again he made notes. "I'm a bit short of copy these days. Maybe I can use this for an editorial called 'Practice Makes Perfect.'"

A few days later. Mason, Hamil and Kendall had to attend district court. All three testified at the murder trial of Dutch Yeager. Mason gave testimony when the cases of Brucker, Nash and Romero came up. And Kendall was the state's star witness against Tucker. "We won't need you in the other cases," McKinzie told them.

The Delmonico, Hamil noticed, was still closed. "What about that fellow De Shon, Sheriff? Is he still in town?"

"He's still around, Barry. He talks of moving on west, maybe clear to the Coast. But he doesn't seem in any hurry about it."

214

At daybreak on the first of October the entire JR crew saddled up to help Kendall and Boyd get started. They pushed the beef drive to and through Bozeman, on past the Fort Ellis gate and made camp at the mouth of Rocky Canyon. When the herd was bedded down Walt gave final instructions. "Don't try to make more'n fifteen miles a day; Rolfe. Where the grass is good don't make more 'n ten, so they can feed a little. No use hittin' Glendive before the twenty-eighth; won't be any track there till then."

In the morning everyone but Kendall and Boyd rode back to the ranch. There they found young Kim Dallas perched on the corral fence, his saddled pony tied nearby. "Here I am, Mr. Rodman," the boy announced eagerly. "You said soon as I could ride out here you'd give me a job."

Hamil looked at his foreman. "I promised him, Walt. How about it?"

Walt nodded tolerantly. "There's a few prairie-dog holes in the meadow, Kim. Tomorrow run ditch water into 'em and drown 'em out. Next day you can ride the pasture fence."

So October began with Kim added to the crew, with the breeding stock held close by ready for storm-feeding, and with Hamil still leaving all operating decisions to his foreman. On the encircling mountainsides the parks of aspen lost their olive green and grew each day more brilliantly golden. Each day Perry Hamil labored like a common hand on his own ranch, each new sunset bringing nearer the inheritance of Barry Rodman. And each day a beef herd, driven slowly by

Kendall and Boyd, moved another ten or fifteen miles farther down the Yellowstone River.

A card mailed by Rolfe at Big Timber came back by stage. It was dated the fifth and showed he'd made sixty-four miles in five days. "He's right on schedule," Walt estimated. "Barring a snowstorm, he's a cinch to make Glendive by the end of the month."

On the second Saturday of October Hamil rode to town. He put himself in the hands of a barber, sprucing up for tomorrow's date at the fort. The barber had all the latest court news. "You heard about the decisions, Mr. Rodman?"

"Only in the Dutch Yeager case. He's due for a hanging. What about the others?"

"Clint Bowers got fifteen years. Brucker and Romero drew five apiece. Tucker drew ten for kidnaping Kendall and Nash got clean off. No one could prove he was anything more than a cook at that Idaho hideaway."

"What about the Charnys?"

"Harboring criminals was all they could pin on Rhonda. So she got off with a stiff fine and a suspended sentence. Right up to the last minute it looked like Chips would get off that easy, too."

"You mean he didn't?"

"Nope. The district attorney wrote the Department of the Interior at Washington to trace a piece of scrip the Targhee Cattle Company used to get title to a quarter section where the house is on the fenced hideaway. It turned up at the Hailey, Idaho, land office. Two endorsements on it; the first made in 1874 by a

216

stranded immigrant to Chips Charny, at a trading store on the Oregon Trail. The second assignment was made in '77, from Charny to Lou Harrison. So the jury figured Charny was in it with Bowers. Chips drew fifteen years, just like Clint Bowers. Not a bad score, I'd say, considerin' six of the gang already took lead poisonin'. Hunker, Jody, Ranny, Hickey, Dakota and Orme."

From the barbershop Hamil went to see Davis & Davis. His October allowance was due. As Ridley Davis gave him a check for one hundred dollars he said brightly: "Here you are, Barry. Looks kind of silly, dribbling it out to you like this. But I've got some good news. You'll only have to put up with it one more month."

"So soon?" Hamil murmured. He'd been prepared to wait till spring.

"The six months required by law," Ridley Davis explained, "in order to let bills and claims be presented, are now up. Your uncle died in April and this is October. All claims are in and paid. The rest is routine. By the fifteenth of November you can take over the estate completely."

Concealing his elation wasn't easy. "Thanks, Mr. Davis." Hamil tried to make it sound casual and unimportant.

The lawyer thumbed him in the ribs. "We speeded it up a little," he confided, "in case you've got any special plans on your calendar. Like prettying the ranch house a little," he added elfishly, "and maybe a honeymoon trip to New York?"

"I have hopes but no plans," Hamil said gravely.

"He crossed to the Laclede and took a room. A big, florid man saw him from the barroom and boomed an invitation. "Come join me, Rodman.""

Mike Lockhart had his cowman's boot on the bar rail and a bottle of rye in front of him. He filled a second glass when the barman slid it to him. "Been wantin' to see you," he said as Hamil came up, "about that offer I made. It still stands. Sixty thousand on the basis of your June tally."

"I'm shipping three hundred beeves," Hamil said.

"So I heard. The way the market is now they'll bring you around twelve thousand. Whatever they bring, we can subtract it from my June tally bid."

"That's fair," Hamil murmured. He sipped his liquor thoughtfully. "I'll give you my answer on November sixteenth — with a string tied to it."

The big man cocked an eye. "Why November sixteenth?"

"Because on the fifteenth I get title to the estate. Until then it's not mine to sell."

"And what's the string?"

"That you also buy my town property. The Rodman Block. It's been appraised at thirty thousand. If I sell the ranch I'll move on to the Coast. If I do that I want to take everything I've got with me and reinvest it out there."

"Humph! Can't much blame you for that, Rodman. I'd want to do the same myself if I was pulling out of Montana." Lockhart brooded a moment. "Thirty thousand, huh? Make it twenty-seven and it's a deal.

218

Forty-eight thousand for what's left of the JR, and twenty-seven for the Rodman Block. Seventy-five thousand in all."

With the estate's bank assets it would total close to a hundred thousand. Just right, Hamil thought, for a neat new start somewhere else. "Your bid's okay," Hamil said, "and I'll give you my final answer on the sixteenth of next month."

"Well shake on it." The cattleman's big hand closed in a hard grip on Hamil's. A moment later he left the bar.

It left Perry Hamil alone with a decision he'd just made and one which had been plaguing him for weeks. His head pulled him one way and his heart pulled him another. His head said: *When you get your hands on that money run fast and far with it.* His heart said: *You can't run unless you give up Lucia.*

Running far and fast would mean covering his tracks, perhaps even changing his name. To win Lucia he must stand pat as Barry Rodman of the JR ranch. His entire appeal to her was in that character. She liked him, but he knew she wasn't yet in love with him. She liked his steadiness, his dependability, his qualities of kindness and loyalty. It would come to her as a shock if she suddenly saw him as a gadabout adventurer, an opportunist cashing in his heritage much as he'd cash chips after a card game.

Hamil's decision, as he stood brooding at the Laclede bar, was *to let Lucia herself call the turn.* He'd ask her to marry him. If her answer was yes, he'd say no to Mike Lockhart. If her answer was no, he'd say yes to Lockhart and move on, his property all in one neat cash package.

The next day was Sunday and he drove Lucia up Rocky Canyon. "What's the latest from Rolfe?" she asked.

Hamil showed her a post card which had come on yesterday's stage. It had been mailed from Stillwater on October eighth. "That puts him a hundred miles down the trail in eight days. Better than a fourth of the way to the rails."

The girl looked at him curiously. "I'm surprised you didn't go along yourself, Barry. After all, it's your cattle that are being sold."

He gave a mock groan. "And ride back on that stage again, all the way from Miles City!"

She teased him a little. "You didn't mind it so much the other time."

"And you know why, Lucia. Having you with me made it fun. Which reminds me, I want you to save a date. A special occasion. Dinner at the Laclede on November fifteenth."

"What's special about it, Barry?"

"It's the day I take over. The estate titles, I mean," Hamil added lightly. "So it rates a celebration. Okay?"

"Okay, Barry. I'll remember." But for the rest of the drive she was quiet and a little tense. He had a feeling she knew what was on his mind and wasn't ready for it yet.

CHAPTER
TWENTY

The next week end was Walt Mason's turn. As he rode toward town, in his Sunday best, Hamil waved him a tolerant goodbye. He felt sure Walt was wasting his time. Walt had kept company with Lucia longer than anyone else and naturally she was fond of him. The man was forthright, modest, gentle, hard-muscled — and with the solid good looks a girl likes to be seen with. Yet what could he offer Lucia Ripley?

What better than some sod-roofed shack on a homestead? Either that or she'd have to share a foreman's quarters on this or some other ranch. How could a girl with dainty tastes, like Lucia, accept any such life as that?

Yet as Hamil passed the JR tool shed that same Saturday afternoon, he heard talk which disconcerted him a little. Kim Dallas was in there, turning the crank of a grindstone while Pony Willard held the blade of a scythe to it. "That's not the way I figure it, Pony." The voice was Kim's.

The next was Pony Willard's. "You got nothin' to go on, kid. You're just guessin'."

"Yeh? She sat up with me, didn't, she, that night I was shot? Off and on she was my nurse for the next four or five weeks. We got pretty chummy, her and I did."

"Chummy? About what?"

"She did a lot of talkin', mostly to cheer me up. It was when nobody figured I'd ever get well, so I guess she thought it didn't matter much what she said. She asked me how I liked Barry Rodman. I said fine. Then she asked me how I liked Walt Mason. I said fine. Then I asked her how *she* liked them. She said fine. Then she added a few words, half under her breath and with a funny little smile. Something about the only trouble with Walt was he was 'too slow to catch cold.'"

"So what?" the choreman demanded.

"So the way I figure it," Kim said, "Walt's been number one with her all along. But he's too all-fired slow. So she's been dating Barry Rodman just to build a fire under Walt, and maybe speed him up."

"You're loco!" Pony derided. "Dribble more water on this grindstone before it builds a fire under this here blade."

Hamil wondered. Could the boy be right? It wasn't likely. What could a kid like Kim know about women?

Yet when Walt Mason returned to the ranch on Monday morning Hamil gave him a searching inspection; to see whether he looked hopeful or hopeless; encouraged or discouraged. "Have a good time, Walt?" Hamil asked him.

"I sure did, Barry. Saturday night we took in a barbecue out at Spring Hill and Sunday we went to church. By the way, here's a card came in from Rolfe. He passed Huntley on the twelfth and he ought to be at

Froze-to-Death by now." The Froze-to-Death stage station was two hundred and forty miles east of Bozeman.

When Hamil rode to town the next week end he was in a determined mood. Maybe Kim had a point — in reverse. Maybe he, Perry Hamil, had been a bit too slow. When a man goes courting week after week, a girl naturally expects him to make progress. Or at least try to. And Hamil had simply been marking time. Maybe she was piqued by it. Kissless dates, if you strung them out, could get monotonous.

By the time he struck Sourdough Creek, some six miles above town, Hamil had made a resolution. He'd stop marking time. Why wait till the big date on November fifteenth? He'd let her know what he wanted tomorrow; or maybe even tonight. This stalemate with Mason had gone far enough. He'd be masterful and take her in his arms . . .

A rider was coming upcreek through the cottonwoods. A tall, gunslung rider with high, dark cheekbones under a tridented sombrero. He had the piercing eyes of a gambler and sight of him tightened every nerve in Hamil's body. The man reined to a stop, a length away in the trail. The gun on his thigh had a well-worn grip and was in a shallow, flapless holster. Hamil was more than glad to be wearing his own. It was his habit to ride armed into town and then leave his gunbelt with the liveryman before driving out to the fort.

"You saved me a ride, Rodman. I was on my way to see you at the ranch." The smile on Harry De Shon's face was a gambler's smile, the kind he'd make, when shoving a stack of blues into a pot.

"To see me? What about?"

"I'm leaving for Frisco about the middle of next month."

"So?"

"I figure to start me a little clubroom out there," De Shon announced. "Clubroom" was the polite name for gambling house.

"Why tell *me* about it, De Shon?"

"To swing it I need a little loan." The Kansan's eyes narrowed slightly, fixing on Hamil's gun hand. "Say ten thousand dollars."

There it was! The thing Hamil had dreaded ever since running into this man at Miles City. The long-delayed recognition had come. And now blackmail!

The laugh Hamil forced had a hollow ring. "I haven't got ten thousand dollars. Or even *one* thousand."

"That's right. But you *will* have on the fifteenth of next month. I'll hang around till then. You can slip it to me in cash on the sixteenth."

Fury burned through Hamil. "And if I don't?"

De Shon sat relaxed in the saddle, his smile more than ever like a pat hand gambler's. "I can't remember your name. But it's not Rodman. All I remember is your face. A young bucko I slapped into the lockup overnight, one time. You want me to tell those lawyers about it? And what about a redhead at the fort?"

Hamil stared at him bitterly. "If I gave you a loan you'd be back for another one; and still another."

De Shon assumed a hurt look. "No I wouldn't. It'll be the last you'll ever see of me. Cross my heart and hope to die."

That child's-play oath gave Hamil his cue. It was the only possible answer. Here in the Sourdough Creek cottonwoods they must gun it out, draw for draw, somewhere during the next ten breaths of time. Perry Hamil, outlaw killer from the border, matching speed against Harry De Shon, lawman killer from Kansas. Each had shot it out many times, always downing his man. But just now Hamil had one advantage. He knew De Shon was De Shon, but De Shon didn't know Hamil was Hamil. The ex-marshal could remember him only as a drunken youngster carousing with trailsmen after a drive up from Texas.

So De Shon could be overconfident, even contemptuous, as he sat relaxed in his saddle, smiling a winner's smile while ten breaths of time ticked by.

"Make it five thousand and it's a deal." Hamil's offer had no sincerity, but was merely to increase the man's contempt.

"Ten." De Shon's smile was now that of a gambler already reaching for the pot.

"After that you'll leave me alone?"

"Sure I will. Cross my heart and hope to die."

"Then *die!*" Perry Hamil's hand flashed as it drew and fired. It was a hip shot, faster than eye could follow.

De Shon's draw was a split second less speedy. As the man's horse reared, snorting, Hamil shot him again. The Kansan pitched headlong to the ground and lay there, face down, arms limp and motionless.

Hamil, bending over him, found him dead.

His brain went into gear. The body mustn't be found on the trail to his own ranch. Hamil dragged it fifty yards offtrail to a thicket. To the same spot he lugged De Shon's saddle, blanket and bridle. All of it he hid under a brush pile, there in the creekbottom woods.

He turned the man's horse loose to graze at will. Then Hamil rode on to Bozeman and put up at the Laclede. With De Shon's blood on his hands he was in no temper to go calling at the fort. Maybe someone had heard the shots. It would fix the exact time of the killing — a time when Hamil was known to have been on his way from ranch to town. If the sheriff hunted up Hamil to ask questions, he didn't want to be found in Lucia Ripley's parlor.

Tonight he'd better keep to himself, watching the street from his room window, hoping the shots hadn't been heard and that the body wouldn't be found for days or weeks. In that case he'd be in the clear. There'd be no reason to think he'd met De Shon on the trail.

The night passed without any challenge. If anyone missed De Shon, there were no inquiries. By Sunday noon Hamil began relaxing. In late afternoon he saddled up and paid a brief call at the fort.

He had to go because he was expected. But Perry Hamil was in no mood to "make progress," as he'd so boldly planned.

Lucia made it easy for him. "Look, Barry." She showed him a card she'd received in the last mail. "It's from Rolfe Kendall. Wasn't it sweet of him to write me? He mailed it at Miles City on the twenty-second."

226

This was the twenty-seventh. It was only sixty miles down the Yellowstone from Miles City to Glendive. "So by now he's earring those cattle. He'll chaperon 'em to Chicago while Mack Boyd comes home by stage."

"Walt says the railroad will give Rolfe a free ticket back," Lucia chattered. "What a time he'll have! Rolfe has never seen a big city before."

Hamil listened to the girl's light talk, ate the ice cream she served him. He wasn't out of the woods yet. Any minute the sheriff, looking for the killer of Harry De Shon, might come knocking at this door. Only the passage of time would make him safe.

There was no knock at the door. Later, in town, McKinzie gave an amiable nod as he passed Hamil on the street. There'd been no alarm from Sourdough Creek. By morning Hamil felt easy again.

But riding back to the JR he made a wide detour around the brushpile which hid Harry De Shon.

CHAPTER
TWENTY-ONE

Many times Rolfe Kendall had heard of the Palmer House, Chicago's finest. He went directly there from the stockyards, after standing by the scales while yardmen of the Clay-Robinson Commission Company weighed the JR shipment.

It wasn't the first time a cowboy had put up there. At this biggest beef market of the world, cowboys were always bringing cattle in from the ranges. Usually their ranches-allowed them an expense account covering one night in town.

Up in his room Rolfe took a bath and put on a silk shirt. Later he stopped at the hotel barbershop for a haircut, shave and shine. He was well worth the second look a cigar counter girl gave him, as he crossed the lobby on his way out to see the town. A bellboy tugged at his sleeve. "Mr. Kendall of Bozeman?"

"Sure thing. What's up?"

"While you were in the barbershop a lady called to see you, Mr. Kendall. She's in Parlor B."

Rolfe found Parlor B. It had a deep carpet, potted palms and a grand piano. A girl with raven hair and sad dark eyes was waiting there. Her delicate, oval face wore the scars of some bitter tragedy.

She was alone in the parlor. "Are you Mr. Kendall of Bozeman?" she asked quickly.

He made her sit down. "That's right. How did you know I was here?"

"I asked at the Clay-Robinson Company. They said you're stopping at this hotel."

He was puzzled and curious. "What made you ask them?"

"I read this paper every week." The girl handed him a copy of the Bozeman *Avant Courier*, printed five weeks ago. It was open at a marked item.

Barry Rodman of the JR is shipping nine cars of beef to Clay-Robinson Commission Co. of Chicago. Rolfe Kendall will go with them and expects to arrive early in November.

"I'm Diane Burgess," the girl said, "of Roanoke, Virginia."

He'd heard mention of Roanoke. "It's where Barry Rodman came from, isn't it?"

"Yes. We were engaged to be married."

"Were?"

"We're not any more. I thought I knew why. I thought he'd simply lost interest — until I saw something in that paper. Look on the other side, Mr. Kendall."

Rolfe turned the paper over and exposed the *Courier's* editorial page. A short, casual article headed "Practice Makes Perfect" was marked with a blue circle.

Rolfe remembered reading it himself. "It came out just as I was leaving with the cattle. What's wrong with it?"

"Read it again, please. It's what made me catch a train to Chicago, hoping to see you here."

Rolfe read it again and could see nothing to get excited about. It merely described the patient, persevering practice of Barry Rodman all through summer and fall, as he'd stood before a target on an outshed wall.

"What about it?" Rolfe questioned.

"Something's missing," the girl insisted. "Something so obvious, I can't see why the editor would leave it out."

"Leave out what?"

"Mention of Barry's handicap. Don't you see? A man practicing with a pistol like that, day after day, awkward at first but finally becoming expert in spite of . . ." She broke off, staring at Rolfe as it became clear he had no idea what she was talking about. "He never told you about it, Mr. Kendall?"

"About what?"

"When he was in the Navy, a shipboard explosion injured his right hand. They had to amputate the index finger."

It stunned Rolfe. The index finger of a right hand. The *trigger finger!* The man who called himself Rodman, who'd bested both Dutch Yeager and Tex Orme in even-break gunfights, most certainly had a trigger finger. And since Barry Rodman himself didn't, the man at the JR couldn't be Rodman.

230

Rolfe rang and had a boy bring coffee to the parlor. Over it he told Diane what he knew about a man with whom he'd ridden a stagecoach from Miles City to Bozeman. "Bozeman swallowed him, hook and sinker. But since he's got ten fingers, he's not Barry Rodman."

Her first reaction was relief. At least it explained why her letters had never been answered. Then relief faded into despair and dread; for if Barry was alive he would surely have been heard from by now.

"When did he last write you?" Rolfe asked gently.

She had the letter in her purse. It had been written at Miles City on June tenth. "It says he had a ticket on a stagecoach leaving the next morning for Bozeman."

"That would be the eleventh," Rolfe said gravely. "I myself caught a stage out of there on the thirteenth. One of the passengers called himself Rodman. We know now he wasn't."

A grimness growing on his face warned her that he knew, or guessed, a good deal more than that. Diane kept her chin level and looked him in the eyes. "If you know the truth, please tell me. I think I can stand anything now."

He gave it to her as gently as possible. "The stage leaving Miles City on June eleventh was raided by a Sioux war party. Everyone on it was murdered, scalped, mutilated. One of them was identified as a Texas outlaw named Hamil. His baggage, pocket stuff, and later his horse, made them sure he was Hamil."

Her eyes were tearless but dead with hurt. "You think he was Barry?"

"It would explain things," Rolfe said. "The man who showed up as Barry had Barry's papers and baggage. He convinced the lawyers and in a week or so he'll be taking over the property."

"We won't let him," Diane said.

Rolfe nodded gravely. "We sure won't. You'd better go back to Bozeman with me and look him in the face. Then you can tell the lawyers he's a fake."

"I'll do anything," Diane promised. Her chin took a firmness.

"There's a train leaving early tomorrow," Rolfe told her. "And I'll wire ahead for stage tickets, Miles City to Bozeman."

Chicago to Bozeman was a long, long way. A long, weary way on one train to St. Paul and on another to Glendive, Montana. A journey of heavy-hearted dread for Diane Burgess, staring out at the bleak Dakota prairies, mile after mile as she moved on toward whatever curtain of mystery hid the fate of Barry Rodman.

Because her purse couldn't afford a Pullman she sat upright, day and night, in sooty chair cars. The young rangeman sitting by her did what little he could to lighten those long, dragging hours of travel. More and more, with each passing mile, he felt a consuming desire to comfort her, to be accepted as her guide and friend. She spoke of questioning a sheriff when they got to Miles City. "Let me see him for you, please," Rolfe begged.

What was that dust on the horizon? "Antelope," Rolfe told her. Farther on they saw buffalo. Blanket Indians squatting on a depot platform made her wince and turn away. Indians had killed the people on Barry's stage. But maybe he wasn't on it, she kept hoping desperately.

End of rails was still at Glendive. There Rolfe bought tickets on a small steamboat for the seventy-mile ride up the Yellowstone to Miles City. He stood at the rail with. Diane as she watched the land go by. Treeless land on either side, brown and charmless, reaching drearily to the skylines. Her face showed disappointment. "I thought there'd be mountains," she murmured.

"Wait till you see Bozeman!" Rolfe exclaimed. "It's something to look at, that Gallatin country. High mountains on four sides; clear, fast rivers with cottonwood groves; and unless you've mowed it for hay, grass to your stirrups in all the bottoms. You can't beat that Bozeman range, Miss Burgess."

"Aren't we being a little formal?" Her fleeting smile was the first she'd given him and it brought a warm thrill to Rolfe.

He took the cue promptly. "Wait till you see the JR ranch, Diane."

Right away he knew he shouldn't have said it. The dull, dead shadows came back to her face and he knew why. The JR ranch was to have been her home, forever and ever, with Barry Rodman. Mention of it brought back the full brutal shock of her loss.

When the boat docked at Miles City he took her to a hotel. "If you'll let me have that last letter Barry wrote,"

Rolfe offered, "I'll check the place he stayed here. And talk to the sheriff."

"If it was Barry . . . you'll find out where they buried him?" The words were like needles in her throat.

"Sure I will. You just leave things to me. And get all the sleep you can, Diane. You'll be sitting up three days and two nights, on that stage to Bozeman."

According to the letter, Barry Rodman had found the hotels here overcrowded and so had checked in at a riverfront rooming house. Its name wasn't given so Rolfe made the rounds of all rooming houses, looking at mid-June registrations. Twice he found the name Barry Rodman, once under the date of June tenth and at another place under the date of June twelfth. Rolfe compared handwritings, using his letter as a basis, and concluded that only the June tenth registration had been made by Barry Rodman.

He next called on the local sheriff. The sheriff heard him to the end. "Want me to wire McKinzie at Bozeman?" he offered.

Rolfe had thought that one through and decided against it. "If the man's Hamil, it might warn him and let him get away."

The sheriff agreed promptly. "You say he's off guard right now. Let him stay that way till you get to Bozeman. There'll be no tight case till Miss Burgess looks at him. When she says he's not Rodman they'll give him the works."

He brought out his records on the stage massacre. Rolfe went over them and saw that only one of the bodies had been unclaimed. That one, identified as

Perry Hamil, had been buried here at public expense. "Did you notice a missing finger, sheriff?"

The officer shrugged. "Why should I? All five victims were hacked up and caked with blood. If a finger was missing, we'd have blamed it on the raiders."

In neither the sheriff's mind nor in Rolfe's was there any doubt that the man buried here was Rodman. "We can disinter him, if you say so," the sheriff offered, "and make sure of it."

Rolfe had thought that one through too. A disinterment would make sensational news for the papers. The story might go by wire to the Bozeman *Courier* and warn Hamil. "Let's wait till we get the other man in jail," Rolfe decided. "Thanks, Sheriff."

When the stage rattled across the river bridge, early in the morning, and turned up the north bank of the Yellowstone, Diane and Rolfe were on it. Although the telling had been hard, he'd given her his own and the sheriff's conclusions. Deep in her heart she must have made the same ones herself ever since leaving Chicago. No other solution made sense. In some strange way a Texas outlaw had managed to change places with a dead man, on this very stage road to Bozeman.

The two other passengers, facing. Diane and riding backwards, were derby-hatted salesmen. One was going to Billings and the other to Fort Pease.

"It'll be a tough ride, Diane," Rolfe warned. This was early Saturday and it would be sundown Monday when they made Bozeman. "We'll get cold nights, this late in the fall, so I dug up a blanket."

235

"Thank you, Rolfe." She sat staring into space with a resigned look and didn't speak again all morning.

The second stop out was Rosebud where they took lunch. The fourth station was Sanders where a new driver came on. After supper a cold damp dark came over the land and Rolfe unwrapped a package. He took a plaid blanket from it and handed it to Diane. "Tuck yourself in and go to sleep."

There'd been no sleep for her the night before and tonight it was the same. A nervous dread rode with her as the stage jolted them with every turn of the wheels.

Twice during the darkness they changed teams. At the second night change they crossed to the south bank of the river and she saw camp lights there. One of the salesmen got off and a soldier on furlough got on.

From Fort Pease they rattled on to the breakfast stop at Pompey's Pillar. In the chill of dawn Diane let Rolfe lead her to the station's eating table. Except for strong coffee everything on it repelled her. Even the soldier complained. "Is this sowbelly all you got, Schwartz? What about some eggs?"

There were no eggs and soon the stage was rolling on. At Huntley, near midday, they crossed to the north bank and low November water made fording easy. Diane looked out at the hub-deep riffles. "Is this where you tipped over, in June?"

Rolfe nodded. "We all got a ducking. Cram, Hamil, the army girl and me. Hamil got real gallant and toted her ashore."

"When I read about it I thought he was Barry. I wrote him and pretended to be jealous . . . And maybe I was." Her strained little laugh had an ache in it.

Today was Sunday, and fried chicken at Huntley was a welcome relief. The station master recognized Rolfe as one of the upset victims. "You remember that town tamer from Kansas who showed up here that night? Fellow named De Shon."

"Yeh, what about him?"

"Piece of wire news came in from Bozeman. They found him hid under a brushpile upcreek from town. Looked like he'd been on the short end of a gunfight."

"Who gunned him?"

"They don't know. He was two weeks dead when they found him."

For another long day and another long cold night the stage bumped on. Changing teams every fifteen miles, taking on a new driver at every third station. Billings . . . Stillwater, Sweetgrass, Big Timber . . . And that next night the girl from Virginia slept. She slept with Rolfe's blanket tucked around her and near morning her tired head, unconsciously, found a rest on his shoulder. He sat breathlessly beside her, thrilled and fearful; thrilled at the touch of her hair on his cheek; fearful that she'd waken and take it away.

There was a spit of snow outside and the blanket wasn't enough. When the cold made her shiver Rolfe wanted desperately to put his arm around her. But he knew she wouldn't want him to. She was like a bride in mourning, a girl who'd lost her lover on this same wilderness stage line . . .

You can't make love to a girl like that, Rolfe Kendall thought, no matter how much you want to. He *did* want to, more than anything he'd ever wanted in his life. Yet he couldn't even let her know he wanted to. Only this one cold night was his, to live out and to remember. A breath of snow came in but he didn't feel it. Every bump that jostled the dear tired head on his shoulder made a crisis for him, lest she waken and sit up straight. But even when they changed horses at Sweetgrass, where Kim Dallas had escaped from the lynchers, she kept sleeping . . . Then on through the night, up the hoof-worn, wheel-cut Bozeman trail.

Beyond Sweetgrass a strange sense of guilt came to Rolfe. She was sitting exactly where Lucia Ripley was, on this same stage five months ago. And his own seat had been Perry Hamil's. Hamil with a single thought in his mind: to trade places with Barry Rodman; to fill Barry's shoes at Bozeman.

And what about himself, Rolfe Kendall? In a sense he was dreaming the same dream; to take Barry's place, to fill Barry's life, not as an heir but as a husband. Even dreaming about it didn't seem right.

Daylight came and she stirred, sat upright rubbing her eyes. "Where are we, Rolfe?"

"It's Monday morning and we're in Gallatin County. See those mountains ahead? Come sundown we'll pull into Bozeman."

238

CHAPTER
TWENTY-TWO

Just before noon of that same Monday, November fifteenth, Perry Hamil presented himself at the law offices of Davis & Davis. Ridley and Wilbur Davis were expecting him, and everything was ready.

Wilbur slapped him on the shoulder. "This is the day, Barry. How does it feel to be a man of affairs? I see you're all dressed up, to celebrate."

"I'm rigged out for a dinner date," Hamil said with a grin. "Do I have to sign any papers?"

"A few. Sign here . . . and here . . . and here." Wilbur pushed papers in front of him and Ridley handed him a pen.

"For an estate of this size," Ridley remarked, "it's the simplest turnover we ever handled. That's one reason we could put it through in only seven months." He handed over two titles and a bank book.

Hamil gave them a careless glance. A deed to the JR ranch with its chattel; a deed to the Rodman Block; a booklet showing a balance in Barry Rodman's name at the local bank.

"It'll be sweetened about twelve thousand dollars, Barry, soon as that check comes in from Chicago. Fact is, we expect it in the next mail. Rolfe Kendall could be on that same stage, if he started home right away."

"We'll deposit it to your credit," Wilbur promised.

It was as simple as that. Hamil went out walking on air. His impulse was to rush to the bank and draw out the money. But it might start talk. And talk could start suspicion. He must wait at least until that extra check from Chicago was in.

At the Laclede he reserved a table for two, for dinner tonight. In the lobby Mike Lockhart hailed him and they went to the bar for drinks. "Don't forget," Lockhart reminded him. "You're to let me know tomorrow."

"You can depend upon it," Hamil promised.

His gambler's mind still clung to a decision. If Lucia said yes tonight, he'd say no to Lockhart. If she said no, he'd say yes to Lockhart. Again it was as simple as that.

Either way I win. His dice-throwing brain kept repeating it over and over. If she said yes he'd win the most beautiful girl in Montana. If she said no he'd win not the girl but a far wider margin of safety. His whole coup would be foolproof, sealed and delivered. He could skip the country with the full stake intact, unencumbered, and no matter what came to light after that they'd never catch him. One side of the dice meant winning at love, the other side meant safe escape with a fortune.

The same gambler's philosophy made him decide to draw a thousand dollars from the bank this very afternoon. It was always well to have a beltful of getaway money, in case of unexpected trouble.

240

To make the withdrawal plausible, Hamil went to each of the town's two jewelry stores and priced diamond rings. The most expensive one was valued at seven hundred dollars and he lingered long over it, promising to stop in for another look tomorrow. Next he went to the stage company's office and asked the price of two through tickets, by stage and train, round trip between Bozeman and New York.

One of the Main Street merchants, as a sideline, kept a small greenhouse in the backyard of his residence, mainly to furnish cut flowers for weddings and funerals. Hamil ordered a box of roses sent out to Lucia Ripley at the post. From there, with a rosebud in his lapel, he went to Fridley's stable to order a rig hitched in front of the Laclede at six o'clock. Everyone knew it meant a date with Lucia.

Gossip always ran fast along Main Street. Barry Rodman, it was whispered, was about to buy an engagement ring and honeymoon tickets to New York. It had reached the bank when Hamil called there at five minutes before closing time. When he saw the knowing smile on the cashier's face he drew out *two* thousand instead of only one.

Hamil was at the Laclede bar when a hostler from Fridley's hitched a rig out in front. It was a team of matched bays with the stable's shiniest top buggy. He could make the three miles to the post in fifteen minutes so Hamil lingered for a while over his drink.

It was well past sundown but not quite dark yet. As he finished the drink the stage from Miles City pulled in, stopping as always in front of the Laclede. From the bar window Hamil looked out with a quick, personal interest as a mailbag was tossed on the walk. A man from the post office picked it up. That bag could have a twelve-thousand dollar check in it from Chicago.

Four passengers got off and Rolfe Kendall was the only one Hamil had ever seen before. One was a young girl who looked weary beyond endurance. She might, Hamil thought idly, be the new teacher they were expecting for the south side school.

He saw Rolfe Kendall carry the girl's baggage inside and stand by while she registered. Then the lobby boy took the girl upstairs. A chance stagemate, Hamil supposed, that Rolfe had been romancing with on the trip. Rolfe himself had gone out and was crossing Main Street with long, brisk strides.

Hamil started out to his own rig, pausing on the walk to light a cigaret. The stage was still there and Alderson of the *Courier*, who regularly met the stage for this same purpose, was asking the driver what passengers he'd brought in. "Rolfe Kendall got back," the driver reported. "Couple of Shields River grangers and some girl from Virginia."

Perry Hamil froze. What girl from Virginia? He looked up the street and saw Kendall disappearing into the sheriff's office. At once Hamil spun about and hurried back into the lobby. He took a furtive look at the registry book. The last name there was Diane Burgess, Roanoke, Virginia.

He was trapped! The game was up. They'd be on him like a howling pack, any minute. McKinzie and Kendall

242

and the Davis brothers. They'd stand him in front of the girl. Barry Rodman's girl! The rig out in front was no good to him now. Only one choice was left — to saddle up and run.

If they caught up with him he'd need his gun. It was in his room. Hamil took the steps three at a time, raced down the hall, unlocked his door, went in only long enough to buckle on his gunbelt.

Then he hurried back down the hall but voices from the lobby made him stop at the top of the stairs. "He just went upstairs, Sheriff. Room 228. But he'll be down again any minute. That's his rig out in front."

"I'll catch him as he comes through the lobby," McKinzie said. "Wilder, bring the Davis brothers over here."

"What about the girl?"

"Kendall says she's all worn out. So let her rest. She can look at him through the bars, later."

It was more than enough for Hamil. He darted along a side hall and down rear stairs to an alley. It was almost dark as he ran east along the alley. In the next block the alley was fronted by a row of Chinese shops and shanties. After passing them Hamil came out on Church Street, which was lampless, and with no buildings except a church, a blacksmith shop and a few log cabins.

In the gloom of Church Street he crossed Main and got a block beyond it. Then he doubled back west two blocks to Fridley's barn. His horse was stabled there. Passing the Office he spoke sharply to a night man who'd just come on duty. "I won't need that rig I ordered. Pick it up at the Laclede."

Without waiting for an answer he hurried down the barn aisle to the stall which held his horse. His saddle was draped on a rack by it. Hamil led the animal into the aisle, bridled it, tossed on pad and saddle. He drew the cinch tight and led the mount to the stable's rear door. As he set foot to stirrup he remembered he'd be riding all night — riding fast and hard. After a dozen miles or so he'd need to rest and grain his horse; it was the only way he could get out of the county by morning.

Fridley's feed room was just inside the alley door. Hamil looked in there and saw bulging grain bags, one of them open and less than half full. He inverted that one and poured oats on the floor until only about ten pounds were left in the bag. This he took to his horse and tied it back of his cantle. His slicker roll was already there. And thanks to a canny precaution of this afternoon, his money belt had two thousand in cash.

Again Hamil raised boot to stirrup, in a rash of impatience to be gone from Bozeman.

"I was afraid you might try this!" The challenge came from barely five steps away.

Hamil whirled about, stood flat-footed by his horse. Framed against the night, just outside the alley doorway, he saw a leveled gun. The gun was aimed at his stomach and the hand holding it was Rolfe Kendall's.

Had he come alone? Or were McKinzie and his crew of deputies close by, surrounding the barn to cut off escape in any direction?

If Kendall was alone there was still a chance. He was only a run-of-the-mill ranch hand with no gun speed to match Hamil's.

A furtive glance over, his shoulder assured Hamil that the front of the barn was quiet and unalerted. The night man, out of sight in the office, didn't know what was going on. Beyond Kendall the starlit alley was empty, voiceless. After a tense moment Hamil was sure that only one threat, Rolfe Kendall, barred his flight.

He fixed his gaze on the leveled gun. "You don't believe in taking chances, do you?" he jeered.

"Not with you," Rolfe admitted. "On an even break you'd beat me a mile, just like you did before."

It puzzled Hamil. He'd never drawn against this cowboy.

"Happened right here." Rolfe reminded him, "at this same doorway back in June. We both went for our guns, not against each other but against Dutch Yeager. And you beat me a mile. You'd do it again, right now, if I gave you a chance."

With an even break yes, but not with Rolfe already aiming a cocked gun. Chain lightning itself couldn't beat a drop like that. Hamil licked dry lips. "You mean you'll drill me if I . . . ?"

"I sure will," Kendall broke in, "if you move that gun hand of yours any other way than up. You've got a rep and I haven't. You left a trail of dead men back of you, down in Texas. I'll let you in on a secret. Hamil. I'm a dub. I'm gun-slow. I never won a gunfight in my life. Except this one." Steel glinted in Rolfe's eyes as he added: "Only way I can win it is like this. Reach up your hands, killer, before I count five."

It was five steps from Rolfe to Perry Hamil. Rolfe counted them, advancing slowly with his cocked gun holding its aim on Hamil's belt buckle.

At the count of four he was only a pace away. At five the muzzle of his gun punched Hamil just above the money belt. "You feel like gambling?" Rolfe asked him.

Hamil didn't. His face had an ashy grayness as his hands reached upward.

Rolfe made him turn around, took the gun from his holster. "Let's go for a walk, killer. They're waiting for you at the hotel."

CHAPTER
TWENTY-THREE

That was Monday evening. Early Thursday morning Ridley Davis drove a livery rig to the JR ranch, as a courtesy to his newest client. She had a brief errand out there. "I want to take them home with me, Mr. Davis."

The lawyer nodded, clucked to his team. She meant she wanted to gather up the more personal effects of Barry Rodman. "I know what they are," Diane said. "I helped him pack that portmanteau myself."

"I remember Hamil getting off the stage with it," the lawyer said with a shudder, "back in June." He'd always shudder at that memory. He'd been completely duped by Hamil, and it would be years before Davis & Davis could live it down.

"Mr. Lockhart wouldn't want them, anyway," Diane said. She'd been told of Mike Lockhart's long-standing offer to buy the JR ranch. Barry's ranch by inheritance. But since Barry had died intestate, without blood kin, the property must go by law to the territory of Montana. In due course the territory would sell it to the highest bidder, which in the case of the ranch itself was sure to be Lockhart.

Late in the morning they drew up at the JR ranch house. Only a Chinese cook was there. All other hands were afield. "But they'll come running," the cook grinned, "when I ring the dinner gong."

"While we wait," Diane said, "I might as well gather up things."

Charley took them to the room which had been Perry Hamil's during the five months of his masquerade.

Sight of an empty portmanteau made Diane cry a little. In a sense it had seemed something like a hope chest, her own and Barry's, as she'd helped him pack it for the long westward journey.

On a table there lay Barry's family Bible. Framed on the wall was his discharge from the Navy. In plain sight were the very clothes he'd worn when he'd kissed Diane goodbye in Virginia. A dozen details of the room made it a showcase of hypocrisy, brazenly posed by Perry Hamil to frame him in the character of Barry Rodman.

Lawyer Davis, grasping at a straw, opened the family Bible to look at names and dates inscribed there. But Diane shook her head. "It's no use. Barry often talked about it. There's not even a second cousin still living."

She picked up a few things and began putting them in the portmanteau. She was on the ragged edge of a breakdown, the lawyer thought. Immediately after lunch he must get her out of here, away from these cruel memories and back to town. He'd reserved a passage for her on next Monday's eastbound stage. After only a week of rest she must travel that long weary trail again.

She took the framed navy paper from the wall and put it in the portmanteau. Then she remembered something ironic and taunting which brought a new shade of bitterness to her voice. "When I helped him pack this bag I put a four-leaf clover in it, for . . ." The last word stuck in her throat but the lawyer knew what she meant. For luck! And no luck had ever been worse than Barry Rodman's.

"I slipped it into the secret pocket," she remembered, "so that it wouldn't be lost . . . so that it would go with him all the way."

"A secret pocket?" Lawyer Davis was still grasping at straws.

"It's on the bottom, with the seam hidden by a strap," Diane said. "You'd never know it was there. During the war Barry's father used it to hide dispatches."

Davis came thoughtfully to the table. "I wonder if Hamil ever found that pocket. If the four-leaf clover's still there, we'll know he didn't."

He turned the portmanteau bottom side up, removed a strap. Even then the seam was barely visible. The lawyer used a penknife to pry into it. He raked out two items — a crumbling clover leaf and one thin sheet of paper.

Ridley Davis took the paper to better light and read it. It was dated June tenth at Miles City, Montana, and was in the handwriting of Barry Rodman. Its opening line was, "Realizing I journey forth, tomorrow, into a wilderness full of hazards . . ."

The lawyer read to the end. Then he turned with a glowing face. "It's a perfectly good holograph will, Diane. Any court will uphold it." He read aloud the last line . . . "all goods and property of which I may die possessed, to my beloved fiancée, Diane Burgess."

Presently a gong rang and the entire ranch crew came in for the midday meal. Walt Mason, Rolfe Kendall, Mack Boyd, Pony Willard and Kim Dallas. Rolfe held a chair for Diane and took the one beside her. Ridley Davis sat at one end of the table, Walt Mason at the other. Chinese Charley brought in soup, beans and beef.

Except for quiet greetings Diane hadn't spoken to them yet. Her strangely preoccupied look, and a flush of elation on the lawyer's face, puzzled both Walt and Rolfe. Certainly there was nothing to cheer about. The imprint of shock and tragedy was still on Diane, as much as ever, but something else was there too. It was like she'd been facing some new, bold decision and had just made it.

There was very little talk. What was there to say at a time like this? Any mention of either Barry Rodman or Perry Hamil would have a sting in it. Mack Boyd said there'd been a fresh snow in the mountains, last night. Kim said he'd just found a new calf in the riverbank brush. Walt said he'd be riding to town, right after lunch.

Charley brought pie and coffee. They were ready to leave the table when Mack Boyd asked: "When's Lockhart taking over, Mr. Davis? He'll have his own crew and so maybe us guys better start looking for jobs."

The answer came abruptly from Diane and gave them a start. "Mr. Lockhart's *not* taking over. Barry's Uncle John always said no to him, and I'm sure Barry would have felt the same way. And so do I."

"We've found a holograph will Barry made," Davis explained. "It leaves everything to Diane."

While they gaped at her she made a plea, humble and irresistibly appealing, to the entire crew. "I won't know what to do with it, though, unless you men help me. I mean run the ranch. That's exactly what I want to do. Won't you please help me?"

The news still had them staring dumbly and she singled them out, one by one. "Mr. Pony Willard, you'll stay on here, won't you, please?"

"You can count on me, ma'am," Pony said.

"And you, Kim? And you, Mack? And you, Rolfe? And I *do* hope *you* will, Walt Mason?"

"Sure we will." Three men, Kim, Mack and Rolfe, gave the answer in a breath. Only the foreman kept silent.

She looked at Walt. "And you, Walt? You'll stay on?"

The foreman's face reddened a little. "I'd like to. But it happens I've made other plans."

"Got yourself another job?" Lawyer Davis suggested.

"Not exactly that," Walt said. "A friend of mine has just bought a little horse ranch over on the Yellowstone. He asked me to run it for him, and I said I would."

"Anybody I know?" Davis inquired.

"Likely you do," Walt said. "He's been a cavalryman all his life and when he retires, a few years from now, he wants to settle down raising remounts for the Army . . . Shucks! I'm not tellin' this right." A ruddy frankness broke through Walt Mason's crude defenses and suddenly his face had a wide, happy grin. "We're supposed to keep it secret for a while but I guess I can't fool you folks. Fact is his daughter and I are gettin' married week after next and we're going to run that place together. So it's up to you, Rolfe, to take over here. How about it?"

Diane followed up promptly. "Will you, Rolfe?"

"Any time you say," Rolfe promised.

"Better make it right now," Walt said. "I won't be much good, next week or two. And right now I'm due in town."

When he was gone, Rolfe called Pony Willard aside and gave his first order as boss of the ranch. The choreman nodded. "That's a dern good idea, Rolfe. Kim and I'll get at it right away." He beckoned Kim and they went to the tool shed.

Mack Boyd rode off to his duties of the day. It left Diane alone with the lawyer and Rolfe Kendall. "Time we're starting back to town, Diane." Ridley Davis looked at his watch.

Again the girl surprised them. "I think I'll stay right here," she decided. "Charley can fix a room for me. Will you have my things sent out, Mr. Davis?"

"Of course. Anything else I can do?"

252

"Yes. Something very important. You told me that John Rodman was buried right here on this beautiful ranch. It's exactly where he belongs and I think Barry should be put beside him. Can you arrange it, please?"

The lawyer agreed at once. Naturally she'd want that. They couldn't leave Barry Rodman far away in a felon's grave, where he'd been laid as Perry Hamil.

Diane turned to the new JR foreman. "Will you show me the place, Rolfe?"

He led her down a path toward the river, where there was a fenced half-acre in a grove of cottonwoods. In it a headstone marked the resting place of John Rodman.

Lawyer Davis spoke a few words to Chinese Charley, then got into his rig and drove away toward Bozeman. And Charley immediately began cleaning up the master bedroom, making it ready for Diane Burgess.

From one of the outsheds came a ring of hammers. By midafternoon Pony and Kim had finished a chore there. "Looks a heap better now, Kim."

"Can't blame Rolfe for not wantin' her to see it," Kim said. They'd stripped a dozen bullet-riddled boards from a shed wall and replaced them with new ones. That target wall was now gone, making one less showcase of hypocrisy to remind them of Perry Hamil.

Pony chuckled. "What do you know about Walt Mason, pullin' a fast one like that? Right out of his hat!"

"Out of his hat nothin'!" Kim retorted. "That horse ranch deal's been cookin' ever since June. She as good as told me about it."

The choreman gave him a sharp look. "You mean that army girl? Why would she tell *you*?"

"I was down with bullet poisonin' and she was sittin' by to cheer me up. One day she said: 'I'm tired of living on army posts, Kim. I'd a lot rather live on a ranch.' 'And raise cattle?' I asked her. 'No, horses,' she said. 'Maybe I can get Dad to . . . ' She broke off right there, and I muffed it. But I don't now. She had this deal cooking all the time, playing Hamil a little just to jog up Walt."

Again the choreman chuckled. "It took dynamite, though, to really get Walt started. Remember Tuesday morning? When we heard what happened to Hamil? Him chucked into jail while Lucia was waitin' for him to come out and take her for a date! For Walt it was dynamite and it like to blew him plumb out of his saddle. He was the maddest man I ever saw, Kim, when he lit out hell-bent for the post."

Kim remembered. "He was plenty mad at Hamil, for givin' her a shock like that; but he was ten times madder at himself for lettin' Hamil beat his time."

"Just mad enough," Pony Willard summed up, "to romp out there and grab her in his arms. Pick up the tools, Kim."

Moving toward the tool shed they saw Rolfe and Diane. The pair stood out of earshot on a grassy knoll, the wind blowing the girl's skirt and hair as Rolfe pointed out landmarks in four directions. Snow-covered landmarks, most of them. Window Rock and Mount Blackmore and Spanish Peaks. Banks of pine with cottonwood creeks reaching out from them like the

254

fingers of a hand. Gallatin Peak and Sphinx Mountain, each with a cap of white touching the blue of the sky. In the opposite direction Battle Ridge and Flathead Pass, along the backbone of the Bridger Range. In between a broad savanna of grass, the best cattle range on earth with the lush valleys of three mighty mountain rivers, the Gallatin, the Madison and the Jefferson, joining to make the still mightier Missouri.

With gestures of pride Rolfe stood pointing them out to Diane. The majestic sweep of the scene seemed to cast a spell over them both.

"What about *them*?" Kim Dallas wondered.

It was a fair question. What about Diane Burgess and Rolfe Kendall? Pony Willard, squinting shrewdly at the pair on the knoll, bit off a fresh chew. "The way I see it," he concluded, "is like this. She's all bruised up. I reckon she's about as bad bruised up as a gal can get. But she's not a day over twenty. Rolfe himself's only twenty-three. Neither one of 'em was meant to live alone forever. So let's just give 'em a little time. Kim, and see what happens."